HER FORBIDDEN ROYAL BOSS

For those who have overcome challenges
by choosing love.

PROLOGUE

A WAIL TORE through the tomb-like silence of the parliamentary chamber of the Sun Palace; it was thin, reedy, insistent. Kadir Aydin, Commander of the Guard and Prince Regent Ikem Eze's right hand, cradled the small bundle from which the wail came forth.

Ikem's jaw locked, tense and rigid. Not a single soldier in the room would meet his gaze.

"Give him to me!"

Kadir stepped forward and surrendered his burden. Ikem dumped the child unceremoniously onto the enormous stone council table. He unwrapped layers of soft muslin and examined the limbs of the little boy.

Not merely a *boy*, if he was to be completely accurate. The infant squirming on the table was the current King of Anwu.

His nephew. And his responsibility.

The baby screamed louder, showing two pearly white teeth, but Ikem was undeterred. "He seems unharmed."

"He was unharmed, sir." Kadir's dark eyes radiated calm, as they always did, although his expression was troubled.

"Then what the hell happened?"

"There was a fire this afternoon, in the south kitchens,"

Kadir said. "As is customary there was a full evacuation, and in the confusion the king was separated from nursery staff. He was taken from his pram by a woman dressed as a maid—"

"And no camera caught her face?"

"It was carefully covered, sir, by a mask. It's not uncommon for staff to wear them if they have a cold or are otherwise ill."

"And then?"

Kadir sighed. "King Adim was replaced by a decoy. When the nursery staff discovered it, we locked down all palace roads. They left the king in an unmarked car close to the west exit."

Ikem said nothing; for one hot then chilled minute he actually thought he might be sick. Kadir waited for a full moment, then spoke again.

"Whoever abducted the child had no intent to injure him. We found clothing, food and toys in the vehicle."

Ikem swore. The fact that there even *was* a vehicle… The fact that somehow, someone had managed to spirit his nephew away from his nursery in broad daylight, and attempted to take the child to God knew where—

He closed his eyes tightly and bowed his head, trying desperately to still the drumming of his heart. Since his brother had died a mere year ago, Ikem had been called upon to leave military service, take the position of prince regent and become the legal guardian of the tiny king.

King.

The thought was simply ludicrous, when one looked down at the fragile little body on the table. He could see the boy's ribs through the thin sleep suit he wore, a faint outline above a rounded tummy. He could understand, privately, why some thought the monarchy should be abolished. This was simply monstrous. Barbaric.

What was worse, the little boy had no one to protect him, save for Ikem.

He touched the infant's chubby cheek gently with the back of his finger; the baby spluttered, then took a deep, shaky breath. Ikem pulled the royal pendant from around his neck and dangled it above the boy's head. Little Adim grabbed for it, then began to gum the five-hundred-year-old ivory chip, as many royal infants had before him.

"Everybody out, except for Kadir," he said tightly. "And get the boy's grandmother." The Dowager Princess Felicité was the little king's only living relative besides Ikem, and she usually took care of him during the day. Unfortunately, she'd taken that afternoon to go to the market with her women, and this had happened.

He did not take his eyes off Adim, even as the sound of fifty-five pairs of hobnailed boots clattered on the tiled floor, or as he heard the door opening, Felicité being called in and then rushing to his side. He did not lift his head even when he felt her hover, smelled the cloying jasmine oil she preferred.

"My lord prince."

"Is your staff completely incompetent?" His voice was cold, and he felt rather than saw the older woman flinch. He looked up, determined not to show her any sympathy. She was standing next to Kadir, wringing her hands. Adim saw her, gurgled and rolled over, happy to see his grandmother. She reached for him.

"Don't touch him!"

She paled.

"Ikem." This was quiet, reproachful, from Kadir, but Ikem didn't care. He picked the baby up, then held the boy against his chest. "It seems like Adim is no safer with you than he was with his mother."

Her face crumpled and he had to fight back guilt—that was fighting dirty, and he knew it. But did no one else but him realize how disastrous this day had almost been? Why were they trying to mollify his anger?

In concession to her feelings, he handed the baby to her after a couple of beats, then crossed his arms.

Aside from showing regret at the fact that the entire situation had occurred, Kadir's face was still unreadable.

"I take full responsibility, sir."

"As you damn well should."

"May I speak?" Kadir said mildly.

Ikem took a deep breath. His anger was already dissipating at Kadir's calm. Before he'd been called upon to become prince regent, he'd pursued a career in the Guard, content to serve the Crown in that way. Now that he was on the throne, he was placed in the curious position of being the ruler of his former supervisor.

"It is apparent," Kadir said, "that this is an inside operation. It was simply too easy to get the boy out. This had to be someone who knows the palace, knows the people inside it and knows exactly how much time it would take before anyone noticed the child was missing."

Felicité gasped, then made the sign of the gods and closed her eyes. Ikem ignored her, keeping his gaze fixed on Kadir. "And?"

"We are currently questioning staff. No one leaves until we have answers." Kadir's dark eyes moved to rest on Felicité. "Ma'am," he said bluntly. "Have you heard from your daughter recently?"

At that, Felicité stiffened. "What are you implying?"

"With all due respect, she is the boy's mother," Kadir

said calmly. "She formed relationships with the staff—*your* staff now. And she knows the palace in and out."

At the mention of his former sister-in-law, the Consort Queen Sabine, Ikem ground his teeth. He had plenty of opinions about the young woman who'd abandoned her infant son after her husband's death. He could not fathom how anyone, especially a new mother, could be so heartless. They'd heard from her once and only once. Ikem returned the message with one of his own that had likely left her eyeballs singed. Heartless, evil woman!

"Why would you think it's her?" he snapped. "She's shown no interest in anyone but herself up until this point."

Felicité's face was red with embarrassment, and she held Adim close as if to shield his small ears from the unpleasant conversation. "I have not heard from her, Commander. I do not think—"

"You may go, Felicité," Ikem said dismissively. "We'll smoke her out if it is her."

Visibly distressed and blinking hard, Felicité left the room.

Kadir suddenly looked every bit his fifty-four years and rubbed his brow. "I apologize, Your Grace. I will get to the bottom of this. But for now…" He paused. "I have a proposal. I'd like to increase the young king's security—"

"The young king," Ikem said quietly and shook his head. The anger was dissipating, being replaced by a feeling of hopelessness. Some mornings he wanted nothing more than to do what his sister-in-law had done and flee. He looked at his nephew's chubby face, however, and he could not.

He knew what it was like to be parentless; if he had any choice in the matter, Adim would never feel that way.

"Ikem?"

At this breach in protocol, Ikem looked up. Kadir's eyes shone with sympathy; he was one of the few that Ikem allowed it from. He sighed.

"What do you suggest, Kadir?"

"Given it's an inside operation, sir, a visible increase in the Guard's presence would only confirm their suspicions and make it harder to flush them out. We need someone unseen, someone who blends in. Someone no one would suspect is guarding the king." He paused. "A woman, sir, is who I would suggest. Disguised as a nanny. She will sleep with him, eat with him, sit with him at public appearances—"

"And when *she's* sleeping, eating, or sitting?"

"I will watch over the king myself," Kadir said quietly. "I already have someone in mind. Do I have your permission, sir?"

"You have it." Ikem let out a breath.

Kadir left, and Ikem, alone in the council room, rested his head on the great table that had served so many kings and princes before him. In his mind he tried his hardest to conjure up the image of his departed brother; he wanted him now, and desperately. There was nothing, however, but the faint chill of an empty room and the gurgle of an infant's voice just outside the door—an infant, who by every estimation, was just as alone as he was. And a voice someplace where he'd buried it deep; a taunting, accusing voice that never was silent.

A voice that reminded him that there was a time he'd wanted to be king, and now fate had handed him the rule in the worst way possible.

CHAPTER ONE

Adama Ohi had never been to the Sun Palace.

She, like most of the residents of the tiny principality of Anwu, never had a reason to. It loomed large and lofty, flanked by snowcapped mountains as distant on the horizon as the setting sun.

As a child, her window faced the mountains, and when the sun rose in the mornings, she often looked up at the obelisk on top of the palace. Covered in tiles laced with beaten gold, it reflected light for miles around. You could not see the palace from the ground, but you could see that light. It acted as a landmark for airplanes and travelers, a landmark for the countries that surrounded it. As a girl, it'd been a symbol of all that was great and good about their tiny kingdom, and the legacies that had been passed down from their Igbo ancestors, decades ago. But then she'd left, joined the army, looking for adventure. When she'd come home, only a few months ago on leave, the palace had never seemed farther away—not until she received a call from a man she hadn't spoken to in over three years.

Kadir, Commander of the King's Guard, though no longer her mentor, was never far from her thoughts. After all, he'd been the one to train her during her stint in the army.

"You have a gift," he'd said with that calm directness

of his. "You're one of the most focused soldiers I've ever seen in my life. Were you a man—"

She was not a man, however, and therefore had no place in the King's Guard. Kadir had done the next best thing—sent her abroad to study under his own friends and contemporaries to complete a grueling program, custom-made just for her. Now at the tender age of twenty-eight, she traveled to places she'd only read about as a child, protecting kings, sheikhs, princes, chiefs, oligarchs. Kadir had set her up with her first few jobs, but she now had a reputation of her own in those circles—so when he called her, she'd been surprised.

"Kadir, His Majesty is a child!" She knew as well as anyone else the tragic story of the former king, the sudden accident and his son, too young to even walk, left as sole heir. Thank God Anwu had such a trusted team of advisers; many other nations would have been thrust into chaos, into civil war.

"Yes. It's…complicated," Kadir had said, a little hesitation in his voice. "Would you come and talk to the prince regent, and myself?" He'd paused before delivering the bait. "The prince regent wishes to honor you with a position as one of his Royal Guard."

She'd almost dropped her phone. "You know as well as I do that the positions only go to men—"

"This is by special dispensation." She heard wryness creep into his voice. "Let's just say that this is a job only a woman can do. And…well… I need you, Adama."

It was those last few words, and not the temptation of the position, that made Adama agree to come. Kadir had never asked her for anything before, and he'd already given her so much. He'd rescued her, really, at a time when she cared little about her own life. If taking this job could help her grizzled commander somehow, she'd do it without hesitation. "Yes, sir."

So…she was here. At the palace, and feeling more apprehensive than she had in a long time.

At the gates, her face was scanned and her name was taken down. After a thorough scrutiny of her ID and passport, she was led to yet another checkpoint, where she was divested of the curved knife she wore strapped to her thigh at all times.

"The commander will be with you shortly, ma'am," a young soldier said, inclining his head. "Please come with me."

Adama recognized his insignia. He was a cadet, probably recently established in the palace. Being sent on Kadir's behalf would be an enormous honor for him.

"What is your name, Cadet?" she asked as they walked. She would be sure to mention him favorably to Kadir.

"Uzo, ma'am."

She committed the name to memory. Just inside the gates, they walked left, down a long tiled passageway shrouded by lush greenery that would fade in upcoming weeks as cooler weather approached. As she normally did when she entered a new place, Adama took note of all exit points, weak spots, vulnerabilities. There was only one passage out that she could see, but the walls on either side were made of gray sandstone blocks, fit together loosely to mimic the old style; very, very easy to scale. She let out a breath, slowly.

She never could relax in a place until she'd worked out a way, in her head, to escape.

"The Obelisk Courtyard, ma'am," said Uzo quietly, and Adama found herself wiping her hands on her thighs. She'd developed quite an intuition over years of training, and now her skin crawled with anticipation that she couldn't explain. The palace was, easily, the most secure place in the kingdom. She should feel no fear.

Still, she shifted her senses to high alert.

"Thank you, Cadet."

He allowed himself a small smile. "The commander will be with you shortly," he said and left.

The palace courtyard seemed designed for serenity. There was a deep pool a few meters wide in which a fountain quietly drained, and the walls and grounds were thick with roses in every shade of white found in nature. Some of them were small and creamy, some large and blush-tinted, some so perfectly symmetrical they did not look quite real. Her fingers itched to touch them but she did not; she'd long ago learned to stifle her impulses. She stood, as befit a soldier of her station, legs slightly apart.

Waiting.

Then her mobile rang, shattering the courtyard's serenity. Adama nearly yelped, dug it out of her pocket. It was sealed in the little silicone bag that prevented her from using her camera but she could still see who it was—

Mother?

Adama's mouth went dry—when was the last time she'd spoken to her mother? There was the slightly strained check-in once a month when her mother called to thank her for the money she regularly deposited into the older woman's account, like a girl of good Anwuan upbringing. There were the birthday calls and the once-a-year call to arrange Adama's travels home on furlough. But random calls in the middle of the workweek? Unheard of. She hoped to God nothing was wrong—

"Mother?" It took her a moment to fumble for her tiny

Bluetooth headset and pop it in. "There. I should be able to hear you now—"

"Hello, Ada." There it was, that childhood nickname that no one else used.

"Are you all right, Mother?"

"Why wouldn't I be?" Her mother's voice was clipped. "*Really*, Ada."

"Where are you?"

"I'm at work." Adama's mother had retired from her job as a professor years ago, and had invested her savings into building a small but cozy youth hostel at the edge of their village. Young people and large families often took advantage of the low prices to take in the orchards and hot springs that brought tourists there every year.

Adama pressed her lips together. "Mother, I'm in a meeting at the Sun Palace—"

"The *what*?" Her mother's voice rose with interest. "Oh, are you practicing for Armada Day?"

"Mother, I haven't done Armada Day in years." Soldiers came from far and wide to take part in the annual celebration in the capital, but Adama had always been away on some job or another. "Kadir asked me to come—he has a job for me."

"At the *palace*?"

"Did you want something specific, Mother?"

"Oh, all right." Her mother was obviously still dying of curiosity, but shifted back to business with her usual matter-of-factness. "You can fill me in later, then. And ironically, I was calling to see if you could perhaps tickle your commander's ear. We have some issues in town, and the militia isn't here, possibly because of the celebration— we've filed official complaints, but—"

"What's going on?"

"There's been an increase in Kijamii citizens coming into town."

Adama frowned. Their small border village had one of the best routes in from the neighboring country of Kijamii, one usually used by tourists coming in to enjoy Anwu's lush greenery and even climate, a veritable paradise during the winter months. "There are always Kijamii citizens coming in, Mother."

"This is different." Her mother cleared her throat. "Town council is worried. The number of citizens doesn't match the number of visas that have been given out at the border, which means they're sneaking in somehow. The hostel is usually only at half capacity this time of year—but I haven't had an empty bed for three weeks. And those are people that can pay. There's been people sleeping on the floor of the train depot—"

"In *Anwu*?"

"Something's going on in Kijamii." Her mother made a sound deep in her throat. "Evictions, for one, according to the people pouring in, and the government is appropriating land. This is unverified, of course—"

"Of course." Kijamii was notoriously private, close-lipped, with a leader who was called a dictator in polite company. "I haven't heard anything about it."

"How could you? You were away in—" Her mother paused.

"Malagda."

"If you say so. Anyway, dear, if you could mention to Kadir that perhaps we could use some assistance here, as the local police are quite unequipped to deal with the situation…"

Well, Adama was certainly ready to believe that. The police force in that provincial town had little to do except stamp visas at the border and rescue the occasional cat from a tree. "Mother, you know that's not how it works."

"Yes, but *he'll* know who to contact."

She supposed that was true. "Okay, Mother—really, I have to go now. I'll tell him."

Finally satisfied, her mother hung up.

Adama was googling about the situation when the man dropped silently down from the wall behind her.

Distracted as she was, Adama's body reacted faster than her head did; she dropped her mobile, twisted out of the way, facing him. He lunged toward her, and instinct took over.

He wasn't very tall—perhaps a couple of inches taller than she—and covered with lean muscle outlined by the sleek black trousers and knit shirt he wore, much like her own. He was as agile as he was fit, and his face was covered by a black mask. The hands that emerged from his knit sleeves were lean and smooth, with long, elegant fingers.

Adama ducked his hand, then parried the next blow with her arm, sliding beneath, twisting seamlessly, gracefully. Her training had taken over; she was smaller than he was, but she was also lighter, quicker, more nimble. He was skilled and well accustomed to combat, but Adama had fear—and the adrenaline that comes with it—on her side.

In a split-second decision, Adama let her body drop hard and fast, then twisted, lifted an elbow and groped for his neck. In a moment she had his head down, plunged into the icy-cold waters of the pond. She'd just found his pulse when she heard a shout and saw Kadir. She fairly gaped; she'd never seen the middle-aged soldier move that quickly in all the years she'd known him.

"Adama, let go!" he shouted.

Adama was startled, but held fast. "He attacked *me*!"

"Adama, *now!*"

Only Kadir could make her obey a command against her better judgment. Reluctantly, she released her assailant, and he came up spluttering, dragging the mask from his face. The man sneezed, spewed water and swore. He looked up and locked eyes with her.

Her breath was quite taken away then, and not just because of the one-on-one combat. The man was, frankly, one of the most magnetic she'd ever seen. The broad shoulders and wide chest she'd been held up against only moments ago were crowned by a face that was as familiar as it was handsome. There was a dimpled chin obscured partially by a close-clipped beard; a firm mouth and narrow dark eyes made all the clearer by a shock of dark hair.

Even coughing, furious and half-drowned, he was absolutely striking. Chiseled.

Royal.

Adama's heart dislodged from somewhere in her chest cavity and pushed hard against her throat. Kadir, whose mouth was twitching wildly, cleared his throat.

"Might I have the honor," he said in a voice that sounded curiously choked, "of presenting Lieutenant Adama Ohi to you, Your Grace. Adama, this is the Prince Regent Ikem Eze—"

Adama couldn't say a word.

"You nearly drowned me," said the prince, then turned to Kadir, a look of utter disbelief on his face, rubbing water off his chin. Drops clung to his short beard, sparkling in the sun, little light-made jewels. "She nearly *drowned* me."

Kadir nodded briefly. "I told you she was the best," he said. His mouth did not twitch and his face was perfectly sober, but Adama could see merriment dancing in his eyes, little flickers of light.

The prince nodded, as if he'd had something confirmed. "Very well. Onboard her." He looked at Adama for the briefest of moments, raking her form with his eyes; his expression was a curious mix of awe and irritation.

"What was that?" she demanded. Her voice was shaking; whether from the fight or the way he looked at her, she had no idea. Her entire body felt consumed with the odd sickish heat one gets after being in the sun too long.

"That was a test." Adama barely registered as Kadir stepped forward, pressing his lips to her cheek in a rare show of affection; her eyes were fixed on Prince Ikem, who was still looking at her, his face now inscrutable. "You, my dear former student, passed it with flying colors."

A test?

"A test that seemed like a good idea when I thought of it." The prince regent's voice was a level baritone, slightly raspy and still sounded a bit waterlogged. "I think I got the worst of it," he added, not entirely without humor.

Heat raced up Adama's face. What the hell was the protocol for this? Was she supposed to *apologize*? And even more confusingly, as the prince regent's brandy-dark eyes flickered over her from crown to feet, the heat in her body increased. It took every bit of self-possession she had not to take a step back.

It had nothing to do with their test. Tests she was used to acing, especially tests that tried her physical limits. This was something entirely different, something foreign and unwelcome, something that tightened her chest and limbs.

Her body was responding to Ikem's scrutiny, and not in the way she expected.

Adama didn't realize how silent the courtyard had become until Kadir cleared his throat. "Perhaps—we should meet inside, sir?"

"Very well." The moment was over as quickly as it'd begun. "I'll see you two shortly."

Ikem turned and left, and Adama released the breath she didn't know she'd been holding.

CHAPTER TWO

After Adama collected herself and wiped her face with a towel that Kadir provided, they left for an audience with Ikem.

Ikem. The prince with the eyes that had made her tremble, a curious mix of fire and control. Her stomach hollowed with nervousness when she went over the moment in her mind. Her body was a *tool*, an instrument seasoned and honed by the discipline she'd put it through for over a decade. It responded to things like—routines. Commands. Things that made sense, not to the inadvertent press and warmth of a man's body, or the intensity of his gaze—

Control, Lieutenant.

This was a job.

The prince regent was the charge.

And the strange, coiling warmth in her belly that was fervently, desperately trying to grow would be crushed before it had a chance to take root.

Kadir, much to her irritation, was no help; he'd been teasing her nonstop since Ikem had left the courtyard.

"You didn't bow properly, Adama."

Adama glared up at him. "You have some nerve—"

"It was *his* idea. He thought it would be a good test of your abilities." Kadir paused at a guard's station to take a slim length of tooled leather, then handed it to her. "You did well. I assure you, he's a skilled fighter. Here's your baby."

Adama's fingers closed round her knife sheath with relief; she felt better already, having her fingers around the smooth handle. She paused to bend and wrap the holster round her thigh, securing it with the leather straps she'd spent hours curing with linseed oil to ensure they'd remain both soft and supple.

"If you hadn't been able to subdue him, he wouldn't have engaged you," Kadir added. "He was impressed."

"*That* was impressed?" She'd not only brought the ruler of an entire kingdom to his knees, she'd also nearly drowned him, and she was fairly sure she'd kicked him in the—

She closed her eyes, briefly. Her old commander took no notice; he stopped in front of a tall, intricately carved set of double doors and tapped.

"Enter," came a tense voice.

Kadir nodded. "Go ahead."

Adama lifted her chin and strode forward with her usual soldier's gait, shoulders back, strides of equal length. It was ridiculous to be afraid, too ridiculous! She pushed open the doors with confidence and walked inside, Kadir one step behind her.

When she saw the interior of the chamber, she froze in surprise.

She'd expected a throne room, or a study, or a library, or something appropriate for a ruler to—*rule* from. This was a medium-size room, painted in calming shades of gray and cream and pale blue. There was none of the dull opulence of the palace, not here; the room looked thoroughly modern. A fluffy rug covered the hard floor; letters of the alphabet marched round the windows and across the walls, flanked by dancing zoo animals. A large rocking horse stood in one corner, and the prince regent stood in the center of the room, a wriggling, gurgling baby in his arms.

Adama's mouth went dry.

The prince regent was no less attractive after his battering; if anything, the ludicrous setting made him look larger, more powerful. His coal-black hair was still wet from his dunking in the fountain, and little drops still sat on the tight coils, twinkling in the light. Adama could see the beginnings of a bruise on his otherwise smooth, copper-tinted skin. His mouth was full and held the sort of sensual tilt that comes from an awareness that one is indomitably, undeniably sexy. There was a bare hint of stubble high on his cheeks and outside the confines of his beard, as if he'd forgotten to shave while contemplating how best to attack unsuspecting women from palace walls.

He looked at her as if he suspected her thoughts; she forced them back into the abyss of her mind, quickly, then dropped her chin to her chest—the way she was supposed to the first time.

"At ease, Adama," Kadir said quietly from behind her, and she felt her body automatically loosen. She tucked her hands behind her back, waited.

"Lieutenant Adama Ohi," the prince regent said as if testing it out. Adama felt something inside her quiver, a flash of liquid heat born of awareness. Her body was humming, throbbing with as much adrenaline as it did when she'd been sparring with him only moments earlier.

What the hell was wrong with her?

Kadir was looking back and forth between them as if something had just occurred to him; his mouth twitched, but his voice was grave. "Adama, His Grace wishes to—"

"She's hired. Here," the prince regent said *very* crossly and thrust the baby into her arms.

Adama shrieked.

"A *baby*?" the woman—Adama—cried out, looking horrified, her military *hauteur* completely dissolved. She juggled Adim in her hands as if she did not quite know what to do with him; the little boy, thinking it was a game, laughed out loud. Adama recoiled and attempted to pass the baby back to Ikem, and he roared in surprise. What was wrong with her? "Lieutenant!"

Adama seemed desperate to get rid of the child. She turned and shoved the little boy in Kadir's arms; the soldier was no better at handling him than she was, but at least he attempted to. "Adama," he said in a soothing voice, shifting his load to his left arm, "there's something about the assignment that I didn't tell you—"

"That's a *baby*."

"Yes. Well—yes. You are to guard the current king, His Majesty Adim Eze." Kadir propped the baby up on his chest, turning him to face Adama. The child was large and healthy-looking, with round cheeks and sienna-tinted skin. A soft riot of dark curls covered his head. He beamed gummily at Adama, who took a *very* large step back.

"Now, Adama," Kadir said reproachfully.

"I don't know anything about babies! I've never held one in my life!" Her eyes narrowed as something occurred to her. "That's why you didn't give me details," she said to Kadir accusingly. "You knew that if you did there was no way I would—"

Prince Ikem had had enough at this point. He strode over to the double doors of the nursery, threw them open and bellowed. "Felicité!"

Moments later the child's grandmother appeared at the door. "What in the name of the gods—"

"Take him," Ikem said tersely, pointing to the baby. Adim was still small, but who knew what he was absorbing from this conversation? As a child, Ikem had been privy to enough palace drama to know how much harm it could cause a child's psyche. Felicité folded Adim into her arms with much more skill than any of them had managed and disappeared from the room.

Ikem's furious eyes then descended on Kadir. "You may leave, Commander," he snapped. "I'll talk to her myself."

"Sir—"

"You seem to have left a *few* things out of the job description when you hired her," Ikem said with biting sarcasm.

Kadir lowered his head deferentially and was gone, and Ikem was left with Adama.

She'd managed to collect herself, at least in body, but her eyes were a dead giveaway. They were angry, embarrassed and stormy. "Your Grace—"

"Quiet," he commanded and took his time to look at her. That would be his pleasure, he decided, since she'd dispatched him so easily in the Obelisk Courtyard. He still burned when he thought of it—was he that out of shape?

It felt good to have her in a place where she'd be the one to squirm.

Lieutenant Ohi was dressed for combat—tight black trousers and a long-sleeved, high-necked knit shirt that clung to her like a second skin. He did *not* linger on her breasts, her hips, both of which were generous despite her lean musculature. Her only adornment was a tiny pin that identified her as part of the Anwu military; her dark hair was braided straight back and the long ends were pinned into a bun. She wore no makeup, but really, she didn't need it. Her skin glowed as if with inner light, her lashes were thick and lush and her mouth was the sort of deep rich color that lipsticks would only obscure. She was as arresting as she had been strong, and he found he had to clear his throat before he spoke. "Your commander spoke well of you, Lieutenant."

She did not reply. She'd finally gotten her face under control, and the eyes that faced forward were blank. He'd learned that technique himself in the military. It was as if you shut off an inner light, that part of you that illuminated your thoughts and feelings.

It was startling to see someone else do it.

"The charge," Ikem said slowly, folding his arms across his chest, "is to serve as personal protector to the king."

"The king is a—baby."

"The king is in danger." He swallowed; it was now his turn to shield his face from betraying any emotion. His nephew had asked for none of this, and the sheer terror that had gripped his heart the day he'd been abducted from this very nursery still churned his stomach when he thought about it.

The little boy had virtually no one except for him, a regent bound tightly to the throne by duty, and Felicité, who was older than she liked to pretend.

Were he that baby, he'd scream and never stop.

This woman need not know any of that; he'd hired her for the muscle and nothing else. He touched a still-tender spot right under his cheekbone.

She has the muscle, all right.

"You," he said, "will guard the king, disguised as his new nanny."

She scoffed. "Your men aren't capable of keeping a child that small safe?"

He felt his nostrils flare—one of his major tells—but she did not know that, and he did not take her bait. "There was an attempt on the young king's life last week," he said in clipped tones, "and we have reason to believe it may have been an inside job."

That caught her attention. She shifted from one leg to the other, which got *his* attention. Her military stance did nothing to hide the sharp thrust of her hips, and his eyes could not help but follow their curve before he snapped them back to her face.

Those hips weren't for fighting him to the ground; he could think of far more pleasant uses for them. And she'd noticed. He watched as her face closed off even more; she very nearly took a step backward, then caught herself, lifted her chin.

Interesting.

"What would you have me do—if I were to accept?" she asked.

He smirked. "Accept, as if you aren't in a gated palace with triple-fortified walls?"

"I walked into it under false pretenses."

"That's Kadir's doing, not mine," he said dismissively.

"He had no right—"

"Are you going to let me answer your question, or are you going to keep talking?"

Adama looked aggravated, but she closed her mouth.

"We need to watch him," he said, "without anyone knowing he's being watched. If indeed he's in danger from someone who is close—"

Adama's face registered understanding. "Then I'm likely to see it."

"Yes." He cleared his throat. "He's mainly cared for by his grandmother, but she is old." Felicité would *kill* him for that description. "Older."

"And his mother?"

"Irrelevant." Ikem compressed his lips against the angry words that wanted to rush forth. Any woman who abandoned her son for mere carnal pleasure possessed a level of casual cruelty that deserved no acknowledgment. "You will be paid double your usual rate. And," he said as Adama began to shake her dark head, "if your post is carried out to my satisfaction, you will be made an honorary member of the King's Guard."

At that, her body stilled completely, and those large, almond-shaped eyes began to glow. Pools, Ikem thought, distractedly dark pools, deep enough for a man to drown in.

"No women are permitted—" she began.

"Except by royal decree," he finished and allowed himself a small smile. "Luckily for you, *I* am royal."

"Permission to look around, Your Grace?"

"Certainly."

Adama covered the perimeter of the room in a few steps; Ikem found himself watching her. She had an elegant gait that was not quite curbed by military rigidness; those hips swayed as if they had a life of their own. She peered up at the windows on the west wall, round and close to the ceiling; in a moment she'd produced a knife from a holster strapped to her thigh, plunged it into a gap between the stone and hoisted herself up in one easy motion. Before a shout of surprise could emerge from Ikem's throat, she was up on the sill, looking down at him with a sort of grim satisfaction. Then she tried the window.

"Unlocked," she announced. "Not to mention that there's no guard outside the room. I saw two exits from where I came, and the drop from this window is surviv-able…"

"Now you're showing off," Ikem groused, staring at the knife sticking out of the nursery wall. Felicité would have a *fit*. "Anwu is the safest country in the world," he added, and the words sounded pompous, even to his own ears. "Get down from there. I'll spot you. The floor is hard."

She chewed her lip for a moment; the gesture made her look curiously girlish. Wordlessly, she leaped down. This time Ikem was ready. The moment she took flight, his arms were out and he intercepted her before she hit the floor.

The minute her body was flush against his, he could smell her skin: the sweetness of honey, the sharp woodi-ness of sandalwood, a softness undercut by steel. Adama's body was as lush as it was strong, and just for a moment, softened against his like melting wax. She made a noise deep in her throat and he stepped away from her as quickly as he could, trapping her wrists between his fingers. They were slender, surprisingly fragile; he could feel her pulse. Something about their position awoke something primal, something involuntary. He saw her lashes flutter, and then she pulled away. There was nowhere for her to go except the wall behind her, and the briefest look of panic crossed her face before she half turned and yanked the knife out of the wall.

The spell was broken; Ikem stepped back. Adama sheathed the instrument and looked past him into the room. She seemed unwilling to meet his eyes. He had to fight an impulse to reach out and touch her cheek, drag his fingers over the skin, see if it was as soft as it looked. Adama was breathing a little harder than her activities called for; she'd been less winded when she'd attacked him in the courtyard.

"Are you all right?" he asked. The words didn't come out at all as he intended. They were slow. Sensual. A reflection, really, of the warmth that was now pooling low in his abdomen. He was appalled at his body's reaction to her, even as he wanted to indulge it more than he'd ever wanted anything in a long time.

Adama's reaction was extraordinary; she jerked back as if she'd been struck, and they both winced when her head hit the wall. Her composure was completely shattered, and she looked, for the first time, angry. So angry that he had to consciously restrain himself from being the one to back down.

"There is nothing wrong with me except I'd like some space!"

He stepped back immediately, holding up his hands. This time she did meet his eyes, and hers were liquid. Heated. Unpredictable. And he was drawn to them, but he'd learned self-control in the same army that had trained her, hadn't he?

"Step down, Lieutenant," he said calmly. "You are understood."

CHAPTER THREE

THREE DAYS LATER, Adama was holed up in the little chamber adjacent to Adim's nursery as he napped angelically in his pram, grimly committing *What To Expect the First Year* to memory.

Even if she hadn't had the promise of a commission with the Royal Guard to tempt her, she'd have done almost anything for Kadir. He'd basically been the one to take the angry, hurting teenager she'd been, hone her talents, teach her discipline. He'd been like a father. He was responsible for the woman she was today, and if he needed help, she'd push aside her misgivings about babies and the puzzle that was Ikem Eze and do it.

As usual, Adama approached her new situation—and her misgivings—with cool efficiency. Yes—yes, she'd been thrown off a little bit initially, but there was nothing she couldn't create a plan for, and the charge of one small child should be no different. Securing the nursery and the nearest exits was easy; she wrote a plan for a new security protocol in a couple of hours, sent it to Kadir.

For the baby, she'd speed-read the top three best-selling books on the subject, downloaded the one with the cover she liked best to her mobile to play on repeat and presented the child's grandmother, Felicité, with a list of things she'd need. The dowager princess had been tasked with *acclimating* Adama to her new position, and was in equal parts rude, impatient and despairing of Adama's ever being able to pull this off.

Not that she could blame her. Adama had none of the softness, or nurturing energy, or whatever it was that drew babies to their nannies like moths to flame. She wasn't worried about the functions of nannying—it was easy enough to feed, diaper, bathe and clothe him. But it was the other things that felt so much less natural. Adama could feel herself stiffen when she had to hold Adim, or when the little boy buried his round, soft face in the space between her shoulder and neck. It was too, too strange; she hadn't had contact with a small child since childish snuggles with her brother too long ago—childish snuggles that she'd banished to the back of her consciousness, too painful to remember.

Children needed affection—they needed touch, according to the book in front of her. But that—that wasn't something she could do. She watched Felicité and Kems, her maidservant, kiss and tickle and play with the little boy with a complete loss of formality, of structure. She was glad they were there.

Even the prince regent had no issues being affectionate—

The prince regent. Adama stopped in the middle of a particularly titillating bit on weaning off pacifiers and caught the tender skin of her inner cheek between her teeth. She hadn't seen the man since their chaotic introduction three days previous, although she'd be lying if she said he hadn't been on her mind. She'd mentally replayed their two encounters over and over—the strength in those long limbs, the anger on his handsome face and finally, something more…primal, possessive, in the way he'd looked at her. He'd never crossed the line, but he *could* have. And she wasn't sure she would have minded.

Layered with her embarrassment at her own unprofessionalism had come other memories. There was the scent of him—rain-soaked earth and spice and soap. His chest, where the baby had nestled, was broad and solid, and she knew perfectly well what that had felt like, pressed to him in the courtyard, the muscles working under his skin. Then there was that face, that finely honed, handsome face, the fury in his eyes replaced by a kind of mocking challenge.

Something unsettlingly like lust pricked at the base of her spine, and she quashed it immediately.

A tap at her door made her slam the book shut and leap to her feet. She was in no rush to have Adim wake and fix those judgmental brown eyes on her, or God forbid, cry. Adama eased the heavy door open a crack with all the care she'd taken during her bomb-defusing final and peered into the small face of Kems, the maid that had been assigned to her. "He's sleeping," she hissed.

Kems shook her head. "You'll have to wake him up, Lieutenant. He has a meeting this afternoon." Her face must have registered confusion, because Kems continued to speak. "The king has to be present at every official meeting of state, ma'am."

That was right. Felicité had mentioned that. "Oh—well—"

"It's with the prime minister, ma'am. She'll be here in twenty minutes."

The prime minister? Adama's eyes must have widened, because Kems's face softened into a dimpled smile. "That's nothing, Lieutenant. He'll be seeing the King of England in a couple of weeks, and you'll be there for that, too."

* * *

The worst part of being an ex-ne'er-do-well, Ikem thought, was dealing professionally with people who remembered him as a complete terror. And there was no one who fit that description better than his current prime minister, formerly Judge Catherine Elimu. Worst of all, most of the country seemed to think *she* was the one who walked on water.

Elimania, they called it on social media. It was enough to put him off his food.

"I used to have a picture of her on my wall at uni," Lieutenant Ohi—*Adama*—confided. She'd just walked into Obelisk Palace library, where Ikem's weekly meeting with the head of state took place on Mondays—a nice way to start the week, he thought sardonically. Adama was wide-eyed, excited; for a minute he considered asking that she be excused. But the king had to be present at these Parliamentary check-ins, and there was no way he could juggle a nine-month-old and talk matters of state simultaneously.

Adama seemed slightly more comfortable with Adim than she had during their last meeting at least, although she handled him rather gingerly. A bulging diaper bag hung off her shoulder, and she had him dangling on her hip in a soft gray sling. She wore a pair of pale pink scrubs that he was sure Felicité had bullied her into, and her braids were pinned close at the base of her neck. She looked every inch a palace nanny. You wouldn't have guessed at the true nature of her work, unless you were eagle-eyed enough to note the rippling muscles pushing against the soft cotton.

Not that Ikem was looking.

Adim saw his uncle and squalled in excitement, but Ikem shook his head. "Not now," he said grimly.

Adama's brown eyes opened a fraction wider, as if that

were possible, he thought somewhat distractedly. "Are you all right, Your Grace?"

"I'm fine. Just wishing this meeting to be over already," he added almost under his breath.

"*I've* never been so excited in my life," she said, and Ikem was startled to see her smile. It transformed her face so completely he found himself smiling back despite himself. He stifled it quickly and replaced it with a roll of the eyes.

"I suppose you're an Elimu fan, like everyone else."

"What, you aren't?" Her voice rose in disbelief.

Ikem rolled his eyes again. "She's fine. I suppose." When he looked back at Adama she was staring at him as if he'd expressed a wish to set bunnies afire.

Ikem sighed. "When I was twelve," he said, "I had the misfortune of sitting next to her at a state dinner. She was only a judge then, and had just married our Tanzanian ambassador—"

"Nathaniel Elimu."

"Correct. She quizzed me on Anwuan history, scolded me for getting the answers wrong and confiscated the Nintendo handheld I'd been playing with. She also asked me if I minded much that I'd inherited my grandfather's ears—"

"No!"

"Yes." A part of Ikem felt gratified when Adama chuckled. He hadn't heard it before, and it lit tiny sparks in those deep brown eyes. "I got even, though. When everyone stood to toast the king I emptied her glass of merlot into her handbag."

"You didn't!"

"On the record, I didn't." His mouth twitched. "She didn't buy it, though. And now she's PM—"

"And you're king."

"Regent," he corrected, but he was still smiling.

Adama shook her head and began to decant her charge from the sling.

"Bring him." Ikem held out his hands, and Adama surrendered the baby after only a moment's hesitation.

Adim wriggled and grinned, his head bobbing with excitement, and Ikem had to laugh despite himself. "Good afternoon, Your Majesty."

Ikem tickled his little nephew under his chin and pulled the best out of his arsenal of funny faces, watching Adama out of the corner of his eye. She looked far more comfortable with Adim's pram and walker than the baby itself, unfolding them deftly. Next, she snapped open a thick blanket, which she lay in a patch of sunlight on the floor. It was a pleasure to watch her work, Ikem thought idly. The lines of her body were graceful, and her movements were lithe and quick. She looked up at him just as his eyes were flickering over the line of her hips—

She raised one eyebrow.

"How have you found the little king?" he asked just a hair too loud for his own comfort. He hadn't been expecting his look to be matched so…confidently.

He liked it. If this were a bar or a social event rather than the stateroom in his nephew's palace, he'd have smirked back.

She shrugged. "He's a baby. He's fine, I suppose."

Ikem frowned a little. There was nothing disparaging in her voice; it was said rather neutrally, but it rubbed him the wrong way somehow, such a casual dismissal of his little nephew.

It's not her job to fall in love with your nephew, he chided himself. It was her job to *protect* him, and she certainly was doing a good job of that. She glanced at him once. "Will you hold him for a moment, sir, while I look around?"

He nodded, jiggling the little boy to his other arm and passing a clinical eye over him. Adim's soft brown skin shone and smelled of the same coconut oil he remembered from his own boyhood. His blue bodysuit featured a giant Tigger on the front, and was spotless, covered mostly by a buttercup-yellow bib. His hair shone even in the dim lighting of the reception room; his cheeks bulged with good health. He grinned gummily at his uncle, and Ikem relaxed.

"Do you not like babies?" he asked.

Adama was on the other side of the room by then, her eyes skimming the four corners, the high beams of the ceiling, made by individual iroko trees twisted round each other in a carpentry technique older than Anwu itself.

"I can't say I ever thought about them either way till now," she answered in that same neutral voice that had bothered him so much. "Do the windows open, Your Grace?"

"Yes. But as in the throne room, there's a trapdoor. Lift the rug next to the marble fireplace."

She did so, and her face smoothed out a little. There was definitely more interest there than had been with Adim, and he didn't know why it troubled him so much. She was his *bodyguard*, for God's sake. *Let it go.*

"You've checked the perimeter, Lieutenant. Take him," he said tersely. "I assure you the prime minister won't try to make off with him."

She came promptly. When she held out her arms for Adim, the little boy strained toward his uncle. Ikem cupped the little boy's cheek in his hand; Adim tilted his head into its warmth. Ikem let out the breath he'd been holding on a small laugh.

If Adim was safe and happy, what did it matter what Adama Ohi thought of babies? Adim wasn't starved for love or affection of any kind. And as long as Ikem was alive and breathing, he never would be. He palmed the back of the baby's soft head, laughed when the little boy wriggled and jerked indignantly, clearly wanting to leap to the floor.

"If I let you go, you'd be sorry. Give it two or three months."

Adim blew a raspberry in response.

Adama was looking openly at both of them. The neutral expression had dissolved into something that was more like curiosity.

"You're very good with him, Your Grace," she said almost humbly.

That was enough to soften Ikem. "He's very much his own person, not just a baby."

"He's right on target with his milestones, and he's eating three small meals a day with milk in between." Adama's voice was quiet. "No screen time and plenty of floor time. Felicité comes to visit him quite often."

"Yeah, she dotes on him." Ikem shifted Adim to his right arm, bringing the baby close to his side. It never failed to amaze him the rush of affection that overtook him whenever Adim was close. For the thousandth time, he swore inwardly to pass a legacy onto Adim that would be untarnished by time. All he had to do was maintain what his brother had already set in place. And seeing Adim's face daily was a living reminder of his only charge, his only focus.

Ikem's exhalation of breath stirred Adim's curls; he looked up, met Adama's eyes. Under the mask of professionalism she wore, there was something else: curiosity.

Her head tilted so subtly he'd have missed it were he not looking at her face so closely. He took in the smooth, dark roundness of her cheeks, the flutter of heavy lashes down to where they cast shadows on her face.

Beautiful, he thought, and it tightened his throat with the unexpectedness of it.

Adama extended her hands for the baby. He handed Adim over and stepped back despite the little boy's straining and whining.

"He'll get used to you," he said briskly. He straightened the knee-length tunic he wore over dark trousers—normal attire for state visits—and not a moment too soon, because a discreet tapping sounded at the door.

"The king is herein." He called out the traditional response and cleared his throat. It had a husk to it that he wanted eliminated before the horrid woman entered.

Elimania!

It had been the hashtag when Adama was a young cadet years ago—and excitement bubbled inside her as Anwu's first female prime minister stepped into the room.

Unlike Ikem, who was dressed in his usual modern slant on traditional clothing, she wore a severely tailored pantsuit in a red just south of true crimson. Her hair was styled in her iconic dark twists, now streaked with gray, and pinned tightly to the top of her head with a shell of Anwuan pearls.

She was frowning—the trademark frown that had launched a thousand memes, had shamed presidents, dictators and kings alike. Her small dark eyes skimmed the room, lingering on the mahogany-and-gold chairs in the center; then her eyes flickered over to Adama, who snapped to attention, remembering what the guard at the door had said. And, seconds later, Catherine Elimu was lowering herself before Adama, so low that she could see where the prime minister's hair was tucked into her comb.

"Your Majesty," she contraltoed.

Oh. *Adim*. Of course.

Adim beamed obligingly and drooled. It was sort of adorable, Adama had to admit.

"Your Grace," Catherine said, turning to Ikem, in much frostier tones.

"Prime Minister," he echoed flatly and held out a hand. Catherine took it and inclined her head down, ever so slightly. "It's a pleasure."

"Is it, sir?"

Ikem's mouth twitched. "This is Adama," he said. Adama, who had been carefully taking in the tension between the two, started so abruptly she nearly fumbled the baby. She noted a quick flash of amusement cross Ikem's face. "She's quite a fan of yours."

"I'm glad someone in the room is." Catherine smiled, and her voice was suffused with warmth. "Glad to meet you, dear."

Ikem and Catherine sat facing each other. The latter tucked her feet out of sight, sitting up ramrod straight, her spine not touching the back of the chair. Adama settled on the floor with Adim and placed the baby carefully on his back. She popped felt finger puppets onto her hand and wiggled them absentmindedly as she listened to their conversation with great interest. Hearing Catherine Elimu in action was definitely the opportunity of a lifetime.

"I hope you're well, Prime Minister."

"Tolerably well, Your Grace."

"Can I offer you anything?" Ikem's voice was veiled, though cordial. "I have tea as usual, Anwuan mountain rooibos that's recently come in, which is a treat. It's impossible to get in the city at the moment."

"Yes, it is." Catherine spoke as slowly and as deliberately as she did in meetings of Parliament. "It's too bad, as it's a favorite of mine."

"We have to certainly make sure you drink your fill, then, and perhaps take some home with you." Ikem leaned over, picked up a mobile phone presumably there for that purpose, typed rapidly and set it down. "On the way."

"You're too kind." Catherine's eyes were glittering. "Do you know, Your Grace, *why* we've been restricted from our own tea?"

"The minister of commerce has informed the palace that there are some issues with importing them."

Catherine laughed shortly. "*Issues.* Delightfully vague, but Ezeghua is always vague."

"Will you enlighten me, then, ma'am?" Ikem's voice was still pleasant, but there was a note of irritation there that wasn't before.

"There are refugees from Kijamii at the border, and they are clashing with the military, obstructing safe passage through the mountains," Catherine said.

Shit. The refugees.

To Adama's credit, she'd shared what her mother had told her with Kadir that first day, and her commander, face unreadable as always, had promised to look into it. But she hadn't followed up with him or her mother. She'd been too busy getting accustomed to her new position. She shifted subtly, tilting a bit closer in their direction.

"Goods need to be redirected by sea, which delays them for weeks and decreases the quality. It's hell on us, because as you know—"

"It's a major domestic product."

"Yes, Your Grace."

Ikem's lips were pressed tight together. Catherine seemed to take this as permission to continue and leaned forward. "The refugees can't be blamed, Your Grace. The situation in their country is out of control, and it grows worse."

Adama saw Ikem's nostrils flare, and her stomach knotted. This was bad.

"I have been in touch with the Mwenye Mlimani regularly, and he says—"

"He is a lying despot."

The word cracked in the air like a shot. It took all of Adama's carefully cultivated self-control not to react. Ikem's eyes darted to her for a minute, and she kept her head down.

Silence reigned for a long moment.

"He is our ally, Catherine," Ikem finally said.

"He has rejected integration into any regional frameworks," Catherine said icily. "He refuses any and all advice from Parliament, or from me. And the Wakijamii are suffering. They're running *away*, Prince Ikem. They're crowding the border villages, and they are straining our resources."

Ikem's lips were pressed together, the only tell in an otherwise immobile face.

"Surely we have the means to take care of a few refugees—"

"Thousands of people displaced by the sorry state of their own country are not *a few refugees*, Ikem. And our silence shows our complicity. A Wakijamii despot should *not* be an ally of Anwu!"

Ikem said nothing; pain strained his face, a muscle jerking in his cheek. Catherine must have seen it, too, because her voice softened. "Your Grace—I apologize for my tone. But you *must* know this—"

"I know."

She leaned back, took a deep breath. Then she spoke again.

"I want to ask Parliament—*formally*—to warn Wakijamii of imminent economic sanctions unless they address the human rights issues in their country."

Adama had to suppress a gasp. Adim was being quiet—for now—but she fumbled for his electric-blue dummy, anyway, and handed it to him. She didn't want to risk missing any of this.

Ikem was quiet for a long moment.

"That seems excessive, Catherine," he said after a beat.

"Excessive!" Indignation took Catherine's contralto up to alto. "It's the best course of action, Your Grace, to ensure that not only they know we're serious, but the world sees that we do not condone such atrocities—"

"*Catherine,*" he said, and tension tightened his voice. "I can't."

"But—Your Grace!"

"In case you haven't forgotten, our king is half Wakijamii."

Both pairs of eyes turned to Adim—much too quickly for Adama to pretend she hadn't been listening. *Damn it.* The little boy half turned on his side, banging his pacifier on the blanket, gurgling happily.

"Adim's existence," Ikem continued quietly, "is a result of painstaking work that my father, my brother and *you* spearheaded."

Catherine blanched. "Your Grace—"

"Even though I was out *gallivanting* in uni at the time, as you so frequently like to remind me, I remember how hard you pushed for that alliance, and what my father did to make it happen. The Mwenye Mlimani's practices were not of concern then, were they?"

"The former Mwenye was different from the one that's there now," Catherine said defensively. "And furthermore—"

"When you pushed my older brother into that *disastrous* marriage—" here, he glanced at Adim again "—the one that left my nephew motherless, Kijamii human rights practices weren't of concern then, were they?"

"Your Grace, may I remind you that things change—"

"And you're up for reelection," Ikem finished and rose to his feet. For a moment he towered over Catherine, who suddenly looked very diminutive and much older. Adama's breath caught in her throat. For the first time, probably since she'd met Ikem in the Obelisk Garden, there was kingship all over him. Adama had spent nearly the last decade seeing men command troops. Hell, she'd practically been raised at Kadir's knee in those early days as a baby cadet. But this—this was different.

The passion in Ikem's voice as he defended his brother's legacy cut deeper than ego alone could account for. Stubborn? Definitely. Misguided? Perhaps. But it was potent. It was the passion of a *ruler,* and it stirred something low in Adama's body that had nothing to do with duty.

She watched the muscle jump in his jaw and felt an unwilling flicker of…something. Admiration?

Or just raw, inconvenient lust?

The feeling, whatever it was, was traitorous, a crack in a fortress. What was it that Kadir had hammered into her for years, about a soldier's place?

You are functional, Adama. A piece of furniture.

She was not supposed to notice the breadth of the regent's shoulders or the way conviction made his voice a low, commanding rumble that vibrated straight through the floor and up her spine. She immediately forced the thought down.

Weak point.

She wasn't talking about the room's security. She was talking about herself.

As if her body's pull to him had been expressed out loud, Ikem glanced her way. It was less than a second, but his heavy-lidded eyes were dark and intense.

His look was a thousand things at once. And in that moment—that minuscule, lingering moment—the fate of Anwu felt secondary to whatever thing waged right here between them. It was something so intense it was like physical touch, and one she felt low in her belly. It felt almost—predestined, this pull to him, as if he was meant to have her here, at his side, to look at him in this way.

Then Catherine spoke, and the room shifted back into focus.

Heat was the first thing Adama felt, suffusing her body so quickly she was grateful for her dark complexion. She looked down at Adim's head, blinking rapidly, not daring to look up again except out of the very edges of her line of vision.

"Please sit, sir," Catherine said.

Ikem did not. That muscle was jerking in his cheek again, and violently.

"It isn't right," she said simply, but much of the fight had gone out of her voice. "And Anwu is beginning to notice."

"Trust me, I know," Ikem said, and he sighed, then sat. He allowed a moment of silence to stare down at his hands, then looked up at Catherine. "I will send a message of condemnation to the Mwenye Mlimani over his actions and encourage him to improve the situation. Publicly. But for now, that's all I can do."

Catherine rose to her feet. "Your Grace—"

"That is *all* I am willing to consider at this time, Catherine." Ikem's face was hard. He rose as well, extended his hand.

The prime minister took it almost absentmindedly; she raised her chin. "Parliament wants sanctions," she reiterated.

"Then it's fortunate that I have the final say, isn't it?" Ikem's voice was cold. "Let's not be hasty to condemn a nation that we were happy to ally with up until this point. And perhaps *you* might consider supporting the monarchy, as you've done so delightfully up until now."

At that, Catherine's face was a study. She straightened imperiously; Ikem did as well. A brittle smile curved her lips upward.

"I'll see you next on Armada Day, I suppose, sir?"

"Indeed you will." Adama saw Ikem's face relax just a fraction. "We're looking forward to the festivities."

Adama did some mental calculations. Yes, Anwu's military festival was in a couple of days and would be her first in-country in over five years. No wonder she'd forgotten the day.

"And the little king?"

"He should make it about a quarter through before he sleeps." They laughed, cordially, though there was still considerable strain in the air.

CHAPTER FOUR

WHEN IKEM COULD not sleep, he ran.

He'd adopted the habit shortly after his brother the king died, and he'd been forced to leave the military. His brain refused to stop even after the business of statecraft had ended for the day, and Ikem often lay awake in his chambers well after dark, wide-eyed and exhausted.

Running helped. It reminded him of the PT drills that had been a part of his life since he'd been an eighteen-year-old cadet. Running steadied him. Relaxed him. The easy rhythm of arms pumping and legs drumming the pavement was to him as effective as a rocking chair was to his young nephew, and he usually ended these late-night runs wrung out, forced to sleep by a body that finally admitted it had been pushed to its limits.

Some men in his position indulged in sex, others in drink; Ikem had no patience for the former or taste for the latter. Besides, his brother had had a weakness for both—and it had nearly destroyed both his marriage and his kingdom. Adim's birth had sobered the former king in his final months, however, and Ikem had no intention of ever being brought to his knees by such mistakes.

How the *hell* had he gotten here? As cool night air rushed into his lungs and pushed beads of sweat out on his forehead, Ikem's thoughts wandered back to simpler days. The days before.

Ikem had gone through every possible rite of passage of a spoiled younger royal son. He'd been the overeager child, hurt when his older brother reached puberty and the Crown bound him to their father in a way that would always exclude Ikem. Some of his earliest memories featured his father and his brother walking away from him. Always together.

Ikem ran a little faster.

Then there came the wild-child days. Sex. Partying. No drugs, thank God; he hadn't cared for how they addled his brain. Flunked exams. Shenanigans of every kind. His father's voice, heavy with anger and embarrassment. Attention. *Finally.* Then came that one dreadful day when he'd gone too far—and then, the military.

Ikem's shoulders went back, as if being corrected by his old commander for the first time. He ran a little faster.

Basic training. Sweat. Sore muscles. A heart unaccustomed to exercise that threatened to beat right out of his chest. And Kadir. A few years younger, his bald head gleaming in the sun, and the faintest glimmer of respect in his eyes when the sore, bullied royal cadet didn't quit. Ikem had seen that respect, seen that acknowledgment of what he could be. And it was that little flicker that transformed him completely.

Gods, how he'd loved the military! He felt physical pain every Armada Day, seeing his ex-comrades with their new pins, new badges. His found family, when his own would have been quite happy to forget he existed. But then they'd died, they'd finally left him permanently, and he—

They remembered you, didn't they? When they didn't have a choice. You can't mess this up, Ikem.

His meeting with Catherine had left a bad taste in his mouth. Her accusatory, judgmental voice—he squeezed his eyes shut briefly, then reopened them before risking tripping, falling, braining himself on the packed dirt. And there was guilt there, too—guilt in knowing that people were hurting. Regardless of whether the Kijamii were under his control or not, they were suffering.

What would the kings before him have done? His father? His older brother?

Except he wasn't a king, was he? His job was to maintain what his brother had built. He wasn't equipped for anything else, was he?

So he ran.

For security reasons the land immediately surrounding the palace was kept clear, and it was on this smooth, hard-packed ground that Ikem ran at night—once, twice, sometimes three times if it wasn't enough.

Tonight he did not pace himself as he normally did; he ran full-on, as if some devil or jinn breathed fire at his heels.

The demons were many. Ruling, being a surrogate parent, sanctions, his openly defiant prime minister—and Adama had been there, too, hadn't she?

Ikem stumbled. *Adama.* Here in the crisp air of an Anwuan night, the young soldier resurfaced like an apparition in the mists of his mind. She gestured for him to come, dared him, smooth brown limbs emerging, striding purposefully.

Ikem pushed a little harder, increased his pace, and he forced himself to retain control, to keep his strides even and smooth. He realized he was thinking of Adama as a distraction from other things. He wouldn't use her in that way.

One. Two. Three. Four.

Ikem started when someone overtook him, like a sprite in a fairy tale, and he knew instinctively, with absolutely no evidence, that it must be her. It was as if his mind had summoned her.

"You!" he shouted, his voice nearly lost to the wind.

She glanced over her shoulder at him; he registered the tail end of a look he couldn't decipher before she was done.

Ikem let out a sound of disbelief that resembled a grunt, feeling his ire rise. He caught up to her quickly.

They ran, and the world faded away to nothing but breath and rhythm and the sound of feet on packed dirt.

Adama might be light and graceful, but Ikem was bigger, stronger and had a powerful gait. He matched her pace easily. Adama glanced at him, then trained her gaze forward, as if he weren't even there.

Well.

They ran together for several minutes, Ikem glancing at her every so often. Adama's lips formed an open-mouthed scowl; it was almost funny. Suddenly, she changed direction and took a sharp left, veering into an arched entrance. Startled, he followed her, then blinked in surprise.

He smelled the flowers before he actually recognized the Obelisk Courtyard, the same place he'd attacked her on that first day, in that ill-fated test of her talents. Adama was running now as if she was fleeing him, light as froth. He drew close, closer than he'd been that night…

The security lights flicked off and, startled, Adama stumbled, and hard.

It was credit to Adama's military training that she did not cry out when she stumbled—she only made a sound that was a little less than a gasp. Ikem hauled her up in one smooth motion. She wasn't heavy, but even if she was he wouldn't have noticed; his senses were absolutely overwhelmed by her.

Clean sweat was layered on top of a delightful fragrance that wafted off her skin; his nostrils flared involuntarily. He was breathing hard now, and not only from the running. This was much more elemental, more banal. She was a mere outline in the velvety darkness of the courtyard, but his mind was filling in the blanks quite accurately, unfortunately.

And she hadn't moved, as if hypnotized by his closeness.

Ikem could see the whites of her eyes in the dark, hear her breathing hard through parted lips. He wanted to speak out loud, but something inside him held it back. Adama wore knit leggings and a tank top of the thinnest fabric imaginable; it molded to her body like a second skin, and he could feel heat radiating from her as palpably as if she'd been naked.

The thought of a naked Lieutenant Adama here, on his terms, made him bite the inside of his cheek.

He dropped her wrist immediately; she rubbed it.

"Are you all right?"

"I'm fine," she said almost curtly.

He cleared his throat. "Adama—" he began.

The quiet was shattered by the night watchman, crying out that it was three, and again, the courtyard was illuminated by soft light. Adama's face, framed by the black knit cap she wore, looked softer than he'd ever seen it, and thoughtful.

He didn't want her to look at him in that oddly penetrating way. He had no idea what she'd find, or what his own expression might give away.

"Where is my nephew?" he asked. His voice was harsher than he'd intended.

She took a step back and blinked. Defensiveness tightened her features.

"Kadir has him. I'll resume with him—later, after my break."

Of course. He'd forgotten she was sharing responsibilities with his old commander.

"Your Grace—"

"Thanks for the run," he said. He no longer wanted to run, though his body was humming with the sort of adrenaline he knew would likely last well into the small hours. It wanted release—a release he could not give.

Adama shifted her weight from one leg to the other. During their conversation she'd reverted to her usual military stance; it made things all around more comfortable, he thought.

"The guard is presenting itself at court tomorrow," he said mildly. Adama, to his irritation, looked as cool as ice cream; he was trying to slow his breathing without it being too obvious. "It'll be quite a busy day for you. Have you ever attended Armada Day as a soldier?"

The corners of her mouth lifted. "I have, but because of my station I was usually outside the palace gates. By the time I'd advanced enough to be in the room I was already outside of the country."

"Well, you'll see it tomorrow. From the dais, as the little king will be present." He frowned. "I'm concerned, though, that you may be recognized—"

Adama shook her head. "Kadir wouldn't let that happen. And it's been a few years since I've been here, sir."

"Indeed."

"Yes. I joined up at eighteen and was here in Anwu

for only three years before working primarily overseas." They'd fallen into step together almost naturally, stretching out limbs that hummed from the exercise.

He did the math. Almost ten years in the military. Impressive, from any standpoint. "And your specialties?" He knew them already, of course, but he wanted to hear her speak in that musical voice of hers. It was soft and sweet, but clipped and businesslike all at once. The juxtaposition fascinated him.

"Security systems and design, grappling and—hand-to-hand combat." There was the tiniest lilt in her voice at the last one, one that made him look at her sharply. Her face was sober as a judge.

"You put that to good use on me the other day."

"Yes, sir." There was definitely amusement there. "I hope to never have to use it for Adim."

"Yes, well." That thought was sobering enough. He was glad to know that his little nephew was safe under Kadir's watch. He tucked his hands behind him. They'd come farther than he thought. The palace loomed far enough in the distance that it made conversation necessary, and Ikem was torn between craving silence—God, he was so *tired*—and wanting to know more about the quiet, limpid-eyed young woman at his side. "I'm sorry for all the unpleasantness this afternoon."

"I don't think that statehood is particularly linear."

A diplomatic answer. He pressed his lips together. "Are you familiar with the situation at our borders?"

She shook her head. "Only a little, sir. I was called from Spain for this assignment."

"I see."

"Kadir would be a much better—"

"Yes, we've a meeting scheduled." Ikem cut her off,

feeling more than a little foolish. Since his brother's and father's deaths he'd been a veritable monk, but his official duties had him making small talk several times a week to women of every age and marital and social status. Why was this one woman making it impossible for him to form a rational sentence?

Because you find her attractive. And God knew he hadn't felt that for a very long time for anyone. His senses had been deadened by loss and grief. But now there were prickles of something he hadn't felt in ages.

Not lust—that burned hot and insistent. This was—desire, perhaps? For connection, not necessarily the warmth of a soft body. It was curiosity about another human being, when his sadness had been his center for so many months.

He was interested. And it was both pleasant and stomach-churning.

"Are you from the capital?"

She shook her head. "A smallish village on the outskirts. My parents have a farm, and my mother runs a youth hostel—do you know the Ceres Mountains?"

"No Anwuan would not."

She nodded. "They've got several acres, right at the base—my grandparents purchased it for pennies in the nineties. My parents are former professors, but they gave it up a few years ago. There's a layer of very stony soil there, but they turned it all over years ago and uncovered this really lush, thick bed of soil. Now it's all green and fresh, just bright and healthy, and the sun streams down over the mountain." She spread her small hands as if they were skimming blades of grass.

"And you joined the armed forces because…?"

There was an infinitesimal pause before she answered.

"I wanted to see the world. And sheep make poor company."

A neat enough answer. He eyed her for a moment. "Did you?"

She lifted her head, and to him it seemed the warmth in her face covered just a flicker of distress, but she smiled, and it dissolved, even if the smile didn't quite meet her eyes. "You did the same, did you not, Your Grace?"

"I?"

"The palace is quite small for three people, so I decided to leave for a place with more space," she quipped.

"Chineke," he muttered under his breath, and he felt heat creeping up into his cheeks. Would his words as a resentful teenager haunt him until he died? "You're not old enough to remember that interview," he said.

"You'll forgive me for saying it, Your Grace—"

"Are you sure I will?" He lifted both brows and side-eyed her.

"—but we're not that far apart in age." Adama relaxed, just a fraction. *Good.* Now he'd resumed control of the conversation. He took a deep breath, filling his lungs with the cool air that would warm to a pleasant glow in the morning.

"Fair enough," he allowed, and he smiled to himself. "I do have a good six or seven years on you in service, though, although you wouldn't know it, looking at your accomplishments."

She lowered her head. "Your Grace is kind."

He shrugged. "It's true. International postings, designing security systems on the side, a master's degree in security management—"

She reached her hands up to cover cheeks that he was sure were hot now. "Kadir talks too much."

"No, I just do my research."

She cleared her throat, obviously eager to move the conversation away from her. "Your reputation in the armed forces is always mentioned as a positive example. Your civil defense service—"

"It's nothing." Was that a touch of judgment in her voice, despite the polite words? He knew the initial thoughts of the public when he'd joined up had been that civil service was a cushy job, an assignment for those without the skill or smarts to do bigger things. The tabloids had been merciless.

But then, he'd started serving. He saw what his fellow servicemen did on a daily basis. And he'd been completely humbled. Rescues, help with natural disasters, medical evacuations—he'd done all of it, and thanks to rigid military norms, he'd been given no preferential treatment whatsoever.

It had taken only a few months of training for him to see how little things like his squabbles with his brother and father had mattered, when faced with the realities of how people suffered every day. And that knowledge had crept into his soul. Softening him. Lowering his defenses.

"Sir?"

Ikem came back to the conversation at hand with a start. Adama was looking at him, curiosity making her own face soft. And he felt heat climbing up his neck again. The hour was late, the grounds were still shrouded in darkness and they were still alone.

He cleared his throat.

"I remember," Adama said thoughtfully, taking a step toward him. It didn't make a significant difference in the distance between them, except perhaps in warmth. His body suddenly felt—not suffused in heat, but pleasantly warmed, as if he were standing before a brazier. "Early on, probably your first year in, you delivered a baby by the side of the road, wrapped it in your jacket—"

Of course she'd remember that rescue. His mouth twitched ironically. It'd been afternoon, the sun high in the sky. The woman had been no older than he was, and very beautiful, her small head and large eyes almost swallowed completely by the soft fluff of her Afro. Her husband had been a wreck, babbling in the passenger seat. Ikem had been on patrol when the taxi driver yelled, panicked, that a woman was going into labor in the back of his car. There wasn't time to wait for the police, the ambulance. Both teams had arrived to find Ikem on his knees, calmly telling the woman to breathe, to bear down.

Yes, take my hand. You're doing just fine, sister. One, two, three—

He'd caught the squirming, wet, whimpering baby. Wrapped it in his jacket. The grateful father abandoned his hysteria long enough to take a picture of the beaming prince holding the newborn, whose red, angry face scowled from the folds of military-issue fleece. Ikem's cheeks had been wet; he'd been so moved by this new life. And that image had been on every Anwuan website the next day, single-handedly changing the playboy prince narrative in less than twenty-four hours. His heart had been so full that day, full with the relief of finding what he was intended to do—

He didn't want to focus on what he'd lost; that never did anything for anyone. Instead, he took a full step back, raised an arm and began to stretch out his humming muscles. The pull produced a tingle so pleasurable it escaped in a sound deep in his throat.

Thirty seconds. Twenty. Ten. His heart rate slowed.

Ikem glanced over after a moment to see Adama doing

the same, her chin lifted and nostrils flared as if to take in the cool night breezes all the more deeply. He tilted his head in her direction; the sexual tension from before had finally dissipated in the floral-scented quiet of the night. Now the air between them hung soft and companionable.

Adama's lips tilted up ever so slightly as the lights flickered yet again. "Recovery drill, sir?"

Ikem felt something in his throat constrict. "Go ahead, Lieutenant."

Her voice took on the clipped quality he remembered so well from PT sessions, calling out the stretches, counting from ten. Ikem relaxed into the routine he'd done so many times. It was reminiscent of other nights he'd spent like this in the company of fellow soldiers, unencumbered by everything that had happened since then.

Without even looking at her, he knew her moves matched his perfectly.

CHAPTER FIVE

Armada Day would require Adama's transformation into a proper Anwuan court woman. Felicité insisted, and Adama relented after two days of argument.

Adama was a proud Anwuan, and one who thought she was well versed in their customs; aside from traveling for jobs, she certainly had never lived anywhere else. Still, the pageantry of the court, viewed from the inside, astonished her. When she was a new recruit, she'd been posted on the outside of the palace, so all she'd ever seen was the parade, while standing at attention till her limbs fell asleep.

In person, Armada Day was quite different from the state assemblies she'd grown up watching on the single fuzzy, outdated television in her father's study. In those days she'd pressed against her twin brother's warm frame as they cuddled against the piles of cushions her mother favored. Her brother had known the court better than she did; he'd always been able to name the members of the royal family other than the king and queen, even down to the cousins of the most junior members, with their full titles. It'd made their father shake his head.

"The boy," he would say dryly, "will either be a brilliant historian, or a celebrity reporter."

Now, dressed in a custom-made gown from a local designer, Adama was standing within those gilt passageways they'd gaped at as children. She felt her throat constrict involuntarily. She would have given it all—this night, this fine gown, even the strength and skill that had gotten her here—for a chance to see her brother again.

Adama was glad, in a strange sense, that she'd given in to Felicité's demands when it came to dress. She knew she looked better than she ever had in her life, and it was, in her mind, a way to honor her second half, her twin who had left her far too soon. Her dress, she thought, was far too impractical for a mere nanny, although she could see that much of the king's household was just as fantastically turned out, if not more.

Felicité's maids had taken her through a series of traditional beauty preparations that involved sweating on hot stones followed by full submersion in a cold pool—"to make your skin glow," a beauty woman explained. In the olden days, she'd have been covered in clay mixed with oil and herbs, lying on rocks warmed by the sun.

She'd then had every bit of hair on her body removed with a thick white paste that reeked of sulfur, and was rubbed with fragrant oils till her skin was soft and polished. A dusting of the finest cam powder covered all impurities, and her lips were painted in a gloss so rich and so red her cheeks heated to see it. They looked soft, swollen, ready to be devoured.

The gown, she thought, was equally ridiculous, and she wished for her comfortable military dress uniform with all her might. The caftan she wore over a thin shimmy was light, sheer and clinging, a finely knit fabric of nearly every green found in nature, and shot through with gleaming threads of gold through which her skin glistened— almost indecently, she protested, till Felicité laughed.

"Modern girl," she said almost indulgently. "This gown is

designed to highlight, not to hide, what the gods have blessed you with. It is the height of fashion!" Her mood had improved considerably once Adama's lean, muscular frame had been exposed to her critical eye. "Thank God your breasts haven't whittled away with that abominable training."

"I've trained under the best in his field—"

"And they have nothing to do with this."

"Won't this be a little awkward, handling a baby in it?" Adama said uncertainly. The neckline dipped dangerously low and wide, and even in her few interactions with Adim it'd been clear how much the little boy could squirm, grab and pull. She had no desire, despite Felicité's feelings, to treat the court to an unimpeded view of her *blessings*.

Felicité waved away her concern. "Chamomile and lavender in his bath," she said airily, "and a slightly thicker preparation of milk in his bottle. The banquet and the competitions don't start till seven-thirty. All you'll have to do is push his pram. He won't move through the entire thing."

Felicité had been right. Adim was tucked far into the recesses of his elegant black-and-gold pram, deep in sleep. He did not even stir when a roar from the court went up as she entered, flanked by Kadir on the right, his second-in-command on the left. Her commander's eyes flickered over her, and his brows rose just a fraction.

"Don't say a *word*," Adama gritted out.

He stifled a laugh with a cough. "I wasn't going to, truly. I was just wondering where your knife is."

She fought back a smile, then tilted her head just enough to indicate the wrap on her head. "And stop talking to me," she hissed. "I'm a nanny, remember?"

"Soldiers don't acknowledge nannies?"

"Not in the King's Guard, they don't. They'll think it's a conspiracy, or worse, a flirtation."

"God forbid." His voice was dry. "There's the host now."

Even with the warning, Adama felt her heart slam up against her ribs when she saw Ikem. He had finally forgone his plain military uniform for the splendor of royal dress—and he did not disappoint, not at all. The knee-length tunic over slim trousers in the finest Anwuan damask hugged his broad shoulders and narrow waist, hinting at the muscles beneath; his chest looked wide and powerful. The blue-and-gold fabric, with traces of dark purple, echoed the thin lapis and gold of the diadem on his head; his skin glowed, a mixture of coppers, golds and siennas, all blended into one length of taut and gleaming skin.

For one traitorous moment, she wondered if the prince regent would find her as beautiful as she did him. The glamour didn't even seem real.

Adama jerked when Kadir pinched her elbow, none too gently. "Bow," he said through his teeth, sounding exceedingly amused. At her outraged look he lifted his eyebrows. "You're a *nanny.*"

Ye gods. That was true. She lowered herself gracefully, then rose. From the look on his face the prince regent was more than a little amused as well, and the way his eyes skimmed her body made her feel a heat that was not altogether tied to annoyance.

"Welcome, Lieutenant," he said in that low, rolling baritone. It was not quite a drawl, and almost musical. She could not pin his accent. It was not altogether Anwuan, not like hers, but it was not quite unfamiliar, either. It reminded her of her parents, but was less affected, less pretentious, more refined.

She liked it.

She did not speak, worried her voice would give her away. Ikem bowed low before the pram, then peered into it.

"The little king sleeps," he said dryly. "Are you armed?"

Kadir pointed at her headgear.

"Ah." His eyebrows lifted. "Smart."

She licked her lips, tasting the sticky sweetness of the gloss Felicité had applied with her own hand. "He is safe with me, sir." There was also a cutlass taped to the bottom of the pram, but he didn't need to know that. She moved to sit with Felicité and the rest of the court women and their children in the finely decorated space to the left; however, both prince and commander shook their heads.

"You come with me," said Ikem and gestured to the dais.

"What? Why?" Startled, she stumbled over the hem of her long dress. In a flash Ikem's hand was at her waist, steadying her, iron-strong.

The contact sent a flash of heat through her body. It was the second time he'd caught her in the past twenty-four hours. Apparently, she couldn't keep her balance around him. He released her almost immediately, though, and Adama's relief was so sharp it was painful.

"Because," Ikem said, "the king presides over Parliamentary banquets. And since this king cries intermittently, eats from a bottle and messes his linens, his nanny comes with me." He leaned down casually, so close that his breath was a warm whisper against her ear, and she shivered, much to her distress.

Then again, it wasn't so much a shiver as an involuntary quiver of her body, one that started where his lips met her skin and ended right between the thighs that were bared by her skirt. It was the type of quiver that preceded something slow, sweet, intense; something she had no right to anticipate, not at all. When his hands had hauled her up, her training screamed at her to break the hold, find a defensive stance. But her body...her body melted.

This is how it starts. The warning was a low whisper at the base of her skull. *This is a breach, Adama.*

"I see Felicité had a good time with you," he said. His eyes were tracing the lines of her gown in a way that made her skin burn. She felt naked under the weight of his gaze, and thrillingly so.

Worse than that alone, she *liked* it. She raised her chin and tilted her body toward him. What was it? Acceptance? Invitation?

The truth lay somewhere between those two words.

She did not dare to speak. Adama knew her voice would betray the tremor that had started licking at the small of her back. Ikem leaned closer under the guise of peering at the sleeping baby. "You look fairly royal yourself, Adama," he murmured against her ear. The distance between them evaporated like mists on the peaks of the Ceres Mountains. And in that second, Adama knew the focus of the day was no longer just on Adim, or on military parades. She now had to survive an evening in the company of a man she was inappropriately, ridiculously attracted to, without making a fool of herself.

Ikem inhaled, tickling Adim's cheek with his fingertip. An excuse to stay closer to her, a smoke screen for those watching. "I smell jasmine."

"It's oil," she said faintly.

He made a noise low in his throat. "It's nice."

Adama forced herself to concentrate by breathing slowly, deliberately, the way she did to calm herself in simulation training when she'd been trapped. One. Two. Three.

The prince regent straightened as servers walked in, bearing cheese, figs, berries and wine.

"Enjoy," he said almost casually.

CHAPTER SIX

It felt oddly right, having her there.

Ikem's eyes flickered over to where Adama sat beside him, for what felt like the hundredth time in just the first hour. And all he could think about in this moment was the freedom of the previous night, the rhythm of their feet on the packed earth, the heat radiating from Adama's body when he'd held her close.

He was supposed to be preparing to command the nation's attention, but his own was still fixed on a soldier who looked at him with an infuriating mix of wariness and something else, something that made the air in any room they shared feel thin and charged.

It was the second time he'd caught her in the past twenty-four hours. It'd be foolish to read anything into it…

Adama had been rattled, too, though professionalism won for the moment. She'd settled herself gracefully on the carved mahogany chair to the left of him and ensured her charge was settled as well. He saw her eyes dart round the hall, reidentifying the exits that she would have been told about and seen in the plans of the room she'd reviewed.

Now that the hall was draped with muslin and screens and other fripperies necessary for such an event, they'd be a little harder to find. He leaned in under the guise of filling her glass with fine wine made from Anwuan grapes, shipped in from the north on a bed of new snow, and spoke quietly next to her ear. He rather liked doing that; the soft shell of it was delicately shaped.

"Don't look now as it will be obvious, but under the rug beneath your feet is a trapdoor," he said quietly, then stifled a grin when she stiffened in surprise. He loved knowing more than know-it-alls. "If anything happens we go down, not forward."

He could feel her testing the floor with a foot. "It wasn't in the plan—"

"No, it wouldn't be." His mouth curved up. "It wouldn't be a very good palace without secret passageways, now, would it?"

He let this register, watching as her color rose, flooding her skin with an even deeper, richer hue. She'd been oscillating between professional coolness and warmth that evening; she was definitely unsettled by their closeness. His admission made her finally turn, finally look at him.

Her eyes were just as lovely as he remembered. They were precisely the type of eyes one wanted half-shut in pleasure, or if open, hazy with lust. Her sooty lashes dropped, showing the lids dusted with malachite-and-gold powder, and she looked up again.

"If I am to protect His Majesty," she said, and her voice was soft, yet urgent, "you must hold nothing back from me."

He shook his head. "That would imply I trust you, and I trust no one. Not when it comes to Adim." He thought for a moment that she would be offended; instead, her eyes darkened with understanding.

"If it makes you feel better, I am being paid enough to ensure my trust," she said after a beat.

He took in a breath, then caught the gleam in her eyes and began to laugh. She did not laugh with him, but she did relax, and after another glance to make sure the baby was happy and warm she tore off a corner of local bread, dipped it in the oil. Adama took very little of the elaborate spread in front of them; she limited her plate to vegetables, fresh fruit and that little bit of bread. She did not touch her wine except for the customary sip to toast the sitting king, and even then, most of her food was left on her plate.

"Is the food not to your liking, Adama?"

She answered without looking directly at him, using the opportunity to spear a bit of pineapple so ripe he could smell it from where he was. "I am used to soldiers' rations, sir, and I do not eat much meat. Such richness would weaken me, and I need to be alert for King Adim."

Ah, yes. His little nephew, and the reason they were both here. He also looked at his groaning plate and felt a prickling of what felt suspiciously like defensiveness. First, she implied he could not protect the young king himself, and now she implied that he was overly indulgent. There was nothing more irritating, he thought, than receiving censure for a job that had been thrust upon him.

Were he not in this position, he and Adama would be comrades. Fellow soldiers. They'd be able to swap training horror stories about Kadir; he'd ask her about her Special Force training. Perhaps he'd even ask her to spar. There had been a hint of that last night, in the garden. However, none of that was possible thanks to his brother, whose disease-ridden body had gone to be with the gods, and thanks to the little boy slumbering peacefully in the pram, close enough for both of them to touch.

Remembering his brother made him lean back, his jocularity gone for the moment.

"Every time I look at him," he said soberly, "I remember he has no idea he hasn't got a father."

He saw a muscle pulse in her throat beneath that smooth glowing skin. For the first time since they'd met she looked at him, really looked at him, without defensiveness or apprehension or reluctant, resentful lust.

"He has you, Prince Ikem," she said simply. "You must not discount that."

Emotion rose and tightened his throat, and he disguised it by taking a long sip from his wineglass. Yes, Adim had him, poor soul, in all his inadequacy. He remembered his brother the king, and Adim's mother, that beautiful, treacherous Wakijamii woman with brown eyes as soft as Adim's. He remembered the tears she'd shed when they'd brought her to court, and the absolute misery on the young woman's face every time he'd seen her.

Not even the birth of Adim made her smile.

Ikem unclenched his jaw before speaking, forcing himself to measure his words, tempering his voice as he did so. Smooth. Easy. Unconcerned.

"Your faith in my abilities is undeserved, but I thank you." He raised his hand toward where he saw Kadir's bulk half-hidden in the shadows. The older man was gesturing at him, and he welcomed the intrusion. There was something about Adama's face that encouraged confidences, despite her stoicism, and that disturbed him even more than his attraction to her had.

"The prime minister would like to pay her respects, sir," Kadir said when he was close enough to speak.

Ikem didn't even bother to stifle a groan. "She's here?"

Kadir shot him a reproachful look. "You know she's here, sir. She was one of the first to arrive."

And yes, she had, in a lemon-colored blouse and wrapper in the same stiff African lace she'd been wearing to state occasions since the eighties. An appropriate color, considering she consistently looked like she'd been sucking on the fruit. Ikem reached behind him for one of the hot scented towels that their attendants kept supplying and wiped his hands slowly, deliberately. "I would be *delighted* to see her."

Kadir nodded, not even bothering to hide the roll of his eyes, and retired from the dais. Ikem glanced over at Adama; the woman's eyes had brightened. "I suppose *you'd* be delighted, too."

She actually grinned at him, the first of the evening, and he was vexed to find himself wanting to laugh. He managed to school his face into something decidedly less pleasant in time for Catherine to approach the dais, and stepped down to greet her as he would any other elder.

"You look well, Prime Minister. Is your husband here? Your sons?"

"He hates these things, and he's retired." Catherine obviously was not there for the small talk. "And my boys are defending your borders, as they always are."

"Please, have a seat. Wine?"

"I'm not here for pleasantries," she snapped. "I wanted you to know that my convoy was delayed significantly by a band of protesters on Palace Road."

"Today?"

"Yes. I suspect your guard told you nothing, so as not to distract you from the drinking and dancing." Here, she shot a withering look at Kadir, whose face didn't move, although the slightest of nods confirmed Catherine's claims. He felt a tightening low in his stomach, but he kept his face bland. He hated it when things were kept from him, and for his prime minister to notice!

Kadir was going to get it later, and from the way the man shifted his stance, he suspected he knew it.

"I'm grateful you brought it to my attention, Catherine," he said simply. "Please sit down. Shall we adjourn to another room?"

She looked surprised—but only for an instant, and she sat, mollified. "No. It would only start rumors we don't need. Is your microphone live?"

He double-checked to make sure and shook his head.

She relaxed—marginally. "The border situation," she said flatly. "People are using today as an opportunity to complain on a national stage, Ikem. The press is there."

"Freedom of speech is welcome in Anwu."

"This has nothing to do with freedom of speech! It's accountability!" Catherine leaned in, her convictions blazing high and light in her eyes. "Ikem—something must be done." She stopped, pressed her lips together. "You're being called sympathetic to a tyrant."

"I've been called worse in my life."

"Ikem, that is different and you know it."

Out of the corner of his eye Ikem saw a press photographer raise his camera discreetly, looking very curious at the heated exchange; he forced himself to relax into his chair. "Our former king spent nearly ten years brokering our relationship, Catherine."

"The former king is dead, and the new king can't even sit up unassisted! Ikem—don't be naive. Since you were young you've insisted on acting with less intelligence than I know you possess!"

"Catherine—"

"Do you know what they're calling you on social media?" Catherine's words were sharp now, barbed. *Ikem the incompetent.*

Even as the words left her mouth and Ikem's face smoothed to granite, he could see Catherine knew she had gone too far. What was less expected was the feeling that he'd been actually hollowed out. The two stared at each other for a long moment; then Catherine stood.

Ikem vaguely registered a flashbulb going off.

"I spoke perhaps too strongly," Catherine said after a long moment.

Well, at least she knew that. Ikem said nothing, just looked up at her.

"Your Grace, I would beg of you to at least reconsider—"

Slowly, deliberately, Ikem turned his back on the prime minister and gestured for Kadir to come.

"See to it," he said coldly, "that the road is cleared within the hour. You," he said to Catherine without looking at her, "make your speech. We will all applaud, and then you may leave."

Catherine's face was tight with worry. "Sir—"

"You've said your piece already, Catherine. I have heard."

CHAPTER SEVEN

IKEM THE INCOMPETENT.

Adama had been warned by Kadir, over and over, that her neutrality would be her greatest asset in this position.

"You must think of yourself as functional," he'd lectured. "Dependable. Solid. And completely neutral. You will have opinions from what you see and hear in the palace, but they must not come to the surface. Your duty is to serve, not in judgment, but in obedience. Leave your biases in the barracks with your personal items."

She had, for the most part, hadn't she? But this—

Anyone with a cell phone and Anwuan citizenship had been privy to Ikem's tumultuous reign. Adama herself, though abroad, could reel off the main headlines without hesitation: Ikem's party days, the expulsions, the pot, the messy affairs with the Nollywood actress, the amapiano singer, the Kenyan YouTuber. His redemption arc when he joined the military, the image seen around the world of him wrapping a baby he'd just delivered by the side of the road in his medic jacket. His ravaged face above his uniform, with the Palace Guard bowing low to him, the day he'd been informed of his father's death. His first clashes with Catherine Elimu.

And now, most recently, his proud, hard face standing

immovably against all of Parliament, while Wakijamii refugees clustered round their borders, crying out for help.

Inhumane, his harshest critics cried. *Ill advised*, even the loyalists whispered. And Adama could not be inclined either way; the pain she'd seen cross Ikem's handsome face at the banquet had stopped those thoughts cold. Before now, he'd been merely a symbol of all that worked—and didn't work—in Anwu.

Now she had access to the man. The man who ran at night in order to sleep; the man who stood by policies that clearly gutted him; a military man who still flinched at well-barbed words.

What she *couldn't* say was that he didn't care.

Adama rolled over on her side. She was far too keyed up from the banquet; Armada Day had been long over, and she'd spent the past few hours tossing and turning. There was no sign of light in the east sky.

She wondered what Ikem was doing. She wondered if he was running. And she didn't want to think about Anwu anymore; her thoughts right now were occupied with its regent.

Adama looked at her watch: barely 4 a.m. and it would be only a few hours before she'd be due to take Adim. She half-rolled, half-jumped out of bed, made some brisk preparations with cold water, a toothbrush and mouthwash, rubbed cream onto her face and hands and slipped out of her room.

The cold of the palace corridors stole breath from her, and she wrapped the thin cardigan she'd pulled over her leggings and tank top close around her body, slipping seamlessly past the night guard, who paid her no attention. She wasn't even quite sure what she was looking for.

She wasn't dressed for running. She wasn't dressed for anything. She wasn't—

"Adama?"

His voice, low and quiet, seemed to fairly rumble off the marble walls, and Adama's insides leaped at the sound, even as her body flushed.

So this is what you were looking for, then. She closed her eyes briefly; then she turned. Might as well admit it, long as she was here.

Ikem didn't even look as if he'd been to bed. He was in his simple uniform, the knit shirt outlining every muscle in his shoulders and arms. The charcoal color made his skin and eyes glow.

"You're up early."

"I had trouble sleeping." She swallowed, then ran the tip of her tongue over very dry lips. "I will relieve Kadir in a few hours, so I thought I'd just—take a walk. Or something."

He nodded and took a few steps toward her. Closer up it was evident that he'd had a hard night as well; there were faint dark shadows on his smooth skin. The chill of the floor seeped up through Adama's slippers; she was suddenly very aware of her déshabillé. She'd never wished for those stupid bubblegum-colored scrubs more. Or a *bra*, for that matter. They stood in silence for a long moment, facing each other; his lashes were long, she registered, almost detachedly. They cast shadows on his cheeks.

Ikem the incompetent. She swallowed.

"I'm just about to have breakfast," he said, "in the King's Terrace. Join me."

"Sir—"

"I'd appreciate your acceptance." His voice was slow. Deliberate.

She inclined her head in a bow, clutching her cardigan together. "Your Grace."

His mouth twitched slightly. "Perhaps you'd like to dress yourself first?"

Perhaps, indeed. She nodded, turned around and practically fled.

This was bad.

Adama, who had memorized most of the palace layout the day she arrived after Kadir had provided her with plans, found the terrace easily and returned with Adim clinging to her neck. The little imp had been wide-awake when she returned to her rooms, roaring at the top of his lungs, and his night nanny and Kadir had only been too glad to hand him over. For the first time since she'd started her position, she was happy to see him awake.

It would be much less awkward dining with Ikem this way.

The King's Terrace was in the west wing of the palace, a semisequestered area intended for use by family and close friends. Aside from the occasional guard, the corridors seemed deserted.

The Sun Palace certainly lived up to its name; every element of its design seemed determined to reflect as much sunshine as possible. During the day, warm light streamed in through windows that lined the hallways from floor to ceiling, and ceilings themselves were high and airy. There was the occasional large pane of stained glass in a strategic area, which sent dancing colors spilling out over creamy tile. It was beautiful, but effortlessly so; fresh and modern, but in a very traditional style.

The King's Terrace protruded from the palace walls and was completely open to the air, a porch enclosed in mesh so fine it could not be seen until one walked up to it. It also featured curtains of the lightest gauze that fluttered dramatically in the breeze. Ikem was seated at a low table, reading something on a tablet and drinking from a white mug. Papers were spread about in front of him, stacks held down here and there by granite paperweights so they wouldn't blow away in the wind.

He looked up.

When she met his eyes even the balmy November air felt warm. He did not smile, but his eyes were curious. Adama blushed, then realized he was looking at the baby, not her, and felt oddly bereft. She did not need Ikem Eze to look at her with any kind of tenderness, and yet…

"Good morning," he said, and she snapped to attention.

"Your Grace." She dropped her head to her chest.

"Lieutenant," he responded. "Please come."

She approached the table, juggling Adim awkwardly, and lowered herself to the solid bench with its multitude of soft cushions. She placed the boy down gratefully as soon as she had balanced, then yelped when he took off crawling like a bolt of lightning, spilling the crystal glass of water at her place as he did so. She grabbed him just in time. "Adim!"

The little boy protested, and loudly, then twisted his body through a series of gymnastics to escape her. A prickle of sweat broke out beneath her arms. Nothing in the three baby books she'd memorized had prepared her for sitting with a child at a breakfast table!

To her discomfort, Ikem looked highly amused. "Having trouble?"

"I'm just fine," she snapped, then yelped again as Adim managed to swipe a soft buttered roll from her plate. "All of this is—developmentally—appropriate."

Ikem pointedly picked up his own piece of fresh-baked bread, spreading wild honey on it with every indication of enjoyment. "Indeed."

Adama would have cursed were it appropriate—and were there not a small child in the room—but instead she pressed her lips together, determined to make the little boy sit down on his bottom. When she finally managed to bribe him with a brightly colored teething ring, something caught his attention and he was off again.

Ikem laughed out loud. "Give me the boy."

"Your Grace—"

"I am his uncle, and you are failing spectacularly. Give him to me!"

Seething and embarrassed, Adama stood and leaned over the table. The little boy seemed thrilled to leave her arms, adding insult to injury, and began to laugh as soon as he was in Ikem's arms. Ikem held him over his head, bounced him once or twice, then said something sharp and guttural to a guard under his breath, who disappeared.

"Relief is coming," Ikem said, settling the baby into the crook of his arm. Adim seemed rather content, nestling against his uncle's broad chest and accepting a piece of biscuit from him, which he gummed happily.

Adama leaned back, feeling quite out of breath.

"Please, eat," Ikem said, gesturing at the spread. Unlike the banquet the night before, the table was loaded with every kind of fruit imaginable, yogurt and fresh greens. "All what you eat. I double-checked with Kadir," he said, answering her next question before she asked it. "You eat like a priest, by the way."

"I don't care for food that weighs me down," Adama said stiffly.

Ikem grunted, and they were interrupted when a woman

came, took the baby, bowed and retreated to an alcove—still visible to both of them.

"That's Felicité's girl and the boy's nanny," Ikem said. "Why in heaven's name did you bring him, anyway? You're his bodyguard, not his nanny—in private, you're welcome to use her."

"Since I'm to be his nanny in public, I thought it best to get to know him, so I won't be a stranger," Adama responded. She was still too flustered to eat; instead, she reached for the pot of tea in front of her, sitting on a stone warmer. The dark rooibos was replete with spices and honey; it was the precious tea that was having so much trouble getting into Anwu. Of course the palace would still have some.

She sipped, closed her eyes. This blend reminded her of home so strongly she half expected to see her mother's face when she opened her eyes.

When she did, all there was was Ikem, looking at her again with that—anticipatory look. She looked right back, ignoring the fluttering in her chest. She was not here to be unnerved by this interim ruler, no matter how he made her feel, or how the soft pinkening light of early morning made him look.

Or how badly she wanted to kiss him.

Ikem ate slowly, methodically; there was fruit on his plate, greens, a boiled egg and grilled white cheese. It was salty and full of delicious, creamy curds. Adama sipped her tea, and the two sat in silence for a moment. It seemed even quieter after little Adim had gone.

"I thank you," said Ikem after a moment, his voice rumbling low in his chest, "for coming. I care very much for my nephew, and you do Kadir and myself a great favor."

Adama was so surprised by his words she nearly

dropped her mug. "I am glad to serve the Crown," she finally said.

"Indeed you are." His eyes flickered down; Adama felt that same heaviness in her breasts that had come at the banquet, except this time, thank God, they were restrained by the very tight bra she wore for training. Her nipples were swelling, pushing against the thick fabric in a way that absolutely distressed her, but at least he couldn't *see*. Not this time. She sat up a little straighter, ensuring that her back did not touch a single one of the absurdly tasseled pillows. She could in no way, shape or form appear to be lounging.

Lust, she told herself. She'd dealt with that before; it wasn't new. This should not be a big deal.

"I was commissioned two years before my brother died," Ikem said and went back to his plate. "I would have made lieutenant commander this year had I not—" He paused.

"Had you not been forced to resign," Adama said softly. A sitting regent could not be an active member of the military, particularly not when the only heir was too young to walk or talk, much less rule.

"Yes."

"Your record was impressive, Your Grace," she said. She did not know why she spoke like this, except a part of her—perhaps that part of her that was still in the garden with him, leaning into his embrace and dizzy from how good he smelled—wanted to comfort him.

He laughed, a crisp exhalation of vowels. "I did what I was supposed to. Nothing impressive about it."

She was quiet for a long moment; the silence was broken only when Ikem stood. "I'm getting a drink," he said and again, gave her one of those conspiratorial half smiles. "Green Speed."

Adama laughed out loud. The recipe had been passed round to generations of soldiers in the service. It included greens, fruit, yogurt and the magic ingredient of local berries, which contained three times the caffeine of coffee beans. Adama limited them to only a couple each week; they were much too addictive, and Adama didn't care to be addicted to anything. "They were the only things that kept me going on PT days."

"Would you like one?"

"Please."

His back was to her, and Adama was free to watch the muscles move in his torso as he put in fruit, yogurt, kale and a few of the berries. "We usually didn't have this much variety when out."

That sounded familiar to Adama. "We used dried fruit sometimes," she said, "and powdered milk. Snow, if we were in the mountains. And a water purification tablet."

She heard the smile in his voice before he responded. "And those damned battery-operated food processors—"

"Kadir hated it when we brought those along." Adama shook her head and paused as the blender went off, creating a smooth dull green sludge from what had been put inside. Ikem poured it on a bed of yogurt, crushed ice and fresh fruit, then turned to hand the whole bit to Adama.

"You look happy," he observed.

Adama felt that familiar heat rise up in her cheeks. "I don't smile that much in general."

He shrugged. "You don't owe it to anyone, but I'm glad I managed one from you."

Against all odds, Adama felt her face heat up again.

"What made you go into the military?" he asked, settling back in his seat. "If you don't mind my asking."

Adama did mind, and for reasons the prince regent

would have no idea about, but she tried her best to answer neutrally. "I was a bit bored at school," she admitted. "And a bit of a troublemaker—I just wasn't interested. My parents were—having a hard time, and I think I just needed some structure. As soon as I joined up, I loved it."

"Under Kadir?" Ikem's eyes grew dark, searching.

"No. He came later, when I joined the Special Forces." Ikem nodded. "Your station?"

"The Ceres Mountains." As far away from her mother's home in the valley as she could get, not that Ikem needed to know that. He waited a moment to see if she had more to say, then spoke himself.

"My parents wished me to be a member of the Palace Guard, but I rebelled. I stayed in civil defense."

Adama's brows lifted. Foot soldiers were referred to rather indelicately as cannon fodder, and the militia were the least prestigious, though their work securing the borders and assisting fire and medical services was important. It was virtually unheard of for a privileged child from a good family to choose that line. Ikem's dark face, however, was...wistful?

"You enjoyed it," she said.

"Best years of my life so far." He placed his drink on the table without tasting it. I would have stayed, had not..."

Had not my brother died. He suddenly looked quite young and much less formidable than he had at their first meeting, and Adama felt a rush of sympathy for him. "Hail, Lieutenant Prince," she said quietly. "We appreciate your sacrifice."

He smiled but his eyes were still far away. "Not everyone does."

At that, Adama was silent.

"Last night…" Ikem's mouth thinned. "I know you overheard our conversation. What did you think?"

Adama grasped for a neutral response. "The protests are peaceful, from what I've heard."

"They are trying to fix what isn't broken, and they're undermining the legacy of their king," Ikem snapped. "If there is anything of Anwu to be left for my nephew, I must preserve it!"

Adama held her tongue. Ikem's color was high, his eyes were blazing so dark the color was nearly obliterated and the tension radiating off his body was so thick it felt as if she'd need to grope past it to make any type of response.

Instead, she bent over her beverage, took a long, ice-crusted sip. It was perfect. She licked her lips.

"It is my honor to serve the Crown," she said simply, a repeat of what she'd said earlier. It was true.

He laughed; the sound was tinged with bitterness. "At least you are able to choose the mode of your service."

Adama felt sympathy prick at her—not for him, per se, seated in the midst of such luxury, but at the fact that Ikem so very clearly would have done something else, had he the choice. She could understand the frustration at lack of choice; most of her life, in one way or another, had felt like that since—

She swallowed, and hard. She had no intention of letting her mind wander to places it had no business going. She was not here to prod at old wounds or to lust after her boss, for that matter; she was here to complete an assignment that would not only give her what she always wanted, but also make history. "I have less choice than you think," she said instead. "But I choose to serve the Crown."

"Even though your mother does not?"

Air rushed into Adama's lungs before reason took over.

Of course she would have been vetted thoroughly before entering the palace walls. Her mother had once been a respected educator, before fate had changed the course of her life.

"She was a bit of a socialist, was she not?" Ikem's voice was slow and deliberate. Adama licked her lips.

"My mother is a proponent of free thinking," she said finally. "And regardless of my loyalties, so am I."

"She is very respected." Ikem finally took his eyes off her, leaning back into the cushions. "My father read quite a few of her publications. She hasn't written in quite some time."

"She is semiretired." From the outside, all the public would know was that her mother had lost a son, and that she'd left teaching soon afterward. People in her community treated her with pity, not with censure, and Adama knew it would be unfair to blame her for having a broken heart. Adama took a long sip to discourage conversation, but Ikem kept going. "Why did she leave the university? She was at the height of her career."

Adama bit back the cry that wanted to slip from her mouth. Ikem had, and quickly, managed to hit upon the one sore spot she had, and resentment for his persistence flooded her. "She…felt she'd done enough. And she was interested in private business," she added as an afterthought.

"Because your brother died."

Why was he doing this? Adama forcibly relaxed her grip on her glass. In Special Forces training she'd been told to learn her "tells," and suppress them. That initially had been difficult for her, but she'd managed. This was the first time in a while she'd had to initiate her training. Breathe. Eyes out of focus. Inner calm. Eyes in focus. Look back at the target.

Adama lifted her chin, then very carefully took a long sip of her drink; it was cool, creamy, with a bitter tinge from the tete leaves and caffeine berries. A hugely upscale version of what was supposed to be commonplace, just like the man seated close to her.

She did not know what game this Ikem Eze was playing, and her heart, despite her outside calm, was beating so hard in her chest she wondered if he could hear it. She did not answer, and Ikem's mouth curved up slightly.

"I am sorry for your loss," he said gently. "I, too, have experienced the same."

Of course. The former king, barely a year in his grave. She'd misinterpreted. Air filled her lungs so quickly she felt slightly dizzy, and she laid the glass down on the table, decidedly no longer hungry. Whether this was a power play or an attempt at sympathy didn't matter; it still hurt like hell.

"It was a dreadful accident—"

Tells be damned. Adama was on her feet in a flash, and the prince regent's eyebrows climbed.

"I would rather that our conversation be limited to the job, Your Grace," she said. Her voice was more strained than she liked, but at least she'd said it.

Ikem showed no surprise, which made her think, angrily, that he'd known exactly what he was doing. "Very well. Lieutenant, sit down."

Adama wanted nothing more than to stalk off and leave him and his kingdom behind, and she supposed he knew it, because he spoke again.

"Please."

She sat back down, clenching her jaw so hard it hurt.

"I did not mean to offend."

She didn't give a damn what he meant. This man was

precisely what was wrong with monarchy; that complete self-absorption left no room for anyone but themselves. She dropped her hands to her sides, fisting them tight.

"I did not mean offense now, or any other time we've spoken." His voice gentled. "You have nothing to fear from me."

So he did plan to acknowledge it. Suppressing her emotions had saved her, and this Prince Ikem, she vowed inwardly, would not be the one to undo years of the hardest work she'd ever done in her life. She swallowed hard and looked up.

The intensity in Ikem's expression stilled her; she felt as if she were encased in ice.

"I'm not afraid of you," she whispered through lips that barely moved.

He smiled. "You have no reason to be."

Adama stood, and this time Ikem let her, standing up as well. He extended a hand. "Thank you for coming," he said as formally as if she were a dignitary of state. "You have my word that I will keep this strictly professional. In all areas."

Adama's anger dissipated in favor of embarrassment as her skin grew hot.

Had he tried to take her there in the garden, in the cool blackness of the first hours of the day, she'd have let him. She'd have let him lower her to the ground, touch the parts of her that ached. Lust was an emotion that Adama wasn't afraid of; but emotions could suffocate you if you let them get out of control.

The fact that her stomach roiled whenever she looked at Ikem too closely—and that his moods affected her— was more worrying.

"I appreciate it, sir," she said. How the hell was that her

voice? It was soft. Wavering. She sounded as if his mouth was hovering close to her neck again, leaving the mark of his lips on her skin. He lifted the hand she held out in return and kissed it, as if she were a courtier or a lady of rank; she inclined her head in response.

"Be well, Adama," he said, releasing her, "and please do not hesitate to ask for anything."

CHAPTER EIGHT

TRUE TO HIS WORD, Ikem avoided Adama. It was simply too dangerous to risk otherwise. If it had only been his body that reacted to her touch, he'd be less disturbed. This was different—she challenged his intellect as much as she aroused him bodily. Not to mention that she'd *seen* him. And he could not have that, not he, a man whose first duty was to the Crown.

Adama herself was quiet these days and unobtrusive. He often saw her moving round the palace, dressed in scrubs, or the loose colorful gowns of the palace staff, hair braided into what seemed like a million tiny braids and pinned, soft and full, to the base of her neck. He wondered what she would do if he laced his fingers through the softness of those braids, wound them round his fingers, tugged. Would she melt in his arms? Would she—

He remembered the banquet and her breasts swaying low and heavy beneath the gold-and-green gown, clearly outlined by the fabric; he remembered the way it'd strained over her full hips and the lean musculature of her legs whenever she'd moved. National dress was intended to showcase the feminine elegance of the woman that wore it, regardless of size or shape; Adama's essence had turned it into something else entirely.

Then he reprimanded himself harshly for thinking thoughts he had no right to have. Adama was entirely wrong, for many different reasons. She was a soldier. She was his subject. And even if those things weren't considered—well… There was a sweet vulnerability that crossed Adama's face sometimes, something that made him wonder. He could ask Kadir about her, but that was forbidden as well. All he knew was that…well…the young woman had suffered loss. She was a self-built fortress of walls so high, attempting to scale them would be a violation of the highest order. And she'd joined the service for the same reasons he had, to deal with pain that would be beaten into submission if it wouldn't come out any other way.

All he could do was avoid her and pray inwardly that she would resolve the matter of his nephew's safety with speed. He would keep his promise and appoint the woman to the Royal Guard, but such a commission did not mean she had to be in close vicinity. There were many assignments that could spring from such a position, and he fully planned to ask Kadir to utilize the most extreme example. He did not run in the evenings, either; instead, he paced his room till he panted, and he counted the hours until the horizon softened enough for him to rouse his staff.

He'd done well, he praised himself.

Tonight Ikem donned a dressing gown and went walking in the halls. It was just after three, and the sheer square footage of the palace would ensure plenty of space for him to cover.

He loved the palace at this time of the night, when the Anwuan dusk had cooled the tiles and the halls were dark, save for flame sputtering in the gold sconces on the walls. The halls were perfectly silent as well. The occasional night guard stood immovable in their corners, as natural a part of the landscape as the tiles and sconces were. Their shadows stretched long and eerie across the pale floors, and Ikem was struck with a memory of being absolutely terrified here as a child. Ghosts frolicked in these hallways, ghosts of his ancestors and other specters, the wild imaginings of a mind that knew no rest.

On an impulse, Ikem turned his feet toward his nephew's room. Adama was off duty at this time, he knew, and the little boy would be fast asleep with his night nurse, one of Kadir's men outside the door. Ikem often peered in to check on them in the small hours, and the old woman never minded. The gods knew she slept too soundly to ever know, anyway. He reached the door of the chamber, paused. No sound came from within.

Ikem punched in the code for the door, then slipped through, making no sound. It took time for his eyes to adjust to the darkness, but when it did he took a surprised breath. On the floor close to the baby's bed lay a small pallet on short legs, a bed suitable for camping or the barracks. On it lay Adama, curled up into a half ball, her head resting in the graceful curve of her arm.

Instantly, he froze. Instinct told him she was close to waking, and likely would have upon the door's being opened, were he not a master of stealth himself. Her face was illuminated by the shaded night lamp in the corner of the room. The spray of stars projected on the high ceiling was meant to give the little one a soothing night's sleep, but now the dim light was gloomy. Adama wore what looked to be an army-issue tank top, and her braids were covered by a bonnet of printed cotton. Not five feet away from the pallet slept Adim, dreaming in his custom-made cot.

Ikem wanted to back out of the room immediately, but

Adama moved, thrusting her limbs out and sighing something in a language he only faintly recognized—the dialect of the outer villages. There was a burble of soft laughter, then a gasp, then a panicked warning and then, a whimper of such pain that his own chest tightened to hear it—

When Adama moaned again he realized she was having a nightmare, and a particularly awful one, if the anguish on her face was anything to go by. Her entire body tensed as if she was in pain, and she reached out a hand, moaning brokenly in that tongue again, so foreign and yet so familiar. She jerked as if the recipient of a blow, and the half ball her body had been in tightened.

He could not take this, not anymore. "Adama," he whispered after a fearful glance at the baby. "Adama!"

It did not take much to break the dream hold on her. She sat bolt upright in the tiny bed, eyes wild with panic. She'd drawn a knife before he took his next breath, but recognition dawned before he had to defend himself, and the weapon was lowered, if not dropped. She took an ugly, gasping breath; even in this dim light he could see her cheeks were wet.

"Adama," he repeated. Her eyes were dull, which alarmed him. "Adama!" He bent and grasped her wrists; she jerked away from him, then pulled the neckline of the tank top upward.

"I could have killed you," she said tonelessly.

"Don't flatter yourself." His heart was pounding. "You were having a nightmare."

"That wasn't difficult to deduce, Your Grace." Her voice was low and gravelly. Embarrassed. Angry. It was also foggy with sleep, and her hand groped at the side of the bed until it encountered a silver thermos. She remained upright, still clutching that damned sheet to her chest, twisted the top off the thermos and took a long sip. He suspected it was as much to steady herself as it was for the refreshment. When she put it down, she scowled.

"What the hell are you doing here?"

He was taken aback by her rudeness, but only momentarily. "This is my nephew's room, not yours," he snapped, "and I could ask you the same."

"I work here."

"Not in Adim's room at night, you don't." He watched, almost fascinated, as she collected herself; he had never seen her so flustered. "Where is the night baby nurse?"

"Mara is ill."

He grunted, unconvinced.

Adama was trying to wipe the dampness from her face discreetly.

A self-built fortress with high walls.

Ikem felt an uncomfortable impulse to comfort her, but of course, he could not. Instead, he watched with a sort of fascination as she took a deep breath, then threw her shoulders back and eased herself from the bed. She seemed determined to act as if everything was normal, but that was impossible. Her eyes darted from his face to his chest, which was bare beneath his open dressing gown. She'd fared worse in her gossamer-thin nightwear; it took all of his military-honed self-control to keep his eyes on her face and not on the skin that gleamed beneath the stretched-out fabric of that flimsy singlet.

When she capitulated and folded her arms over her breasts he felt as if he'd won, although he wasn't sure quite what. He tightened his own dressing gown, cleared his throat. "You were moaning. Not with pleasure, I might add."

Her face grew angry. "You—"

"And you're already feeling better. Come, take a walk with me."

Her jaw sagged before she caught it. "Now?"

"Yes." Ikem shrugged. "In the military they used to tell us to clear our heads after a nightmare."

"Or run," she said, somehow managing to lift both her chin and her eyebrow simultaneously.

"Yes… But neither of us is dressed for that." Especially her, with her thin nightwear. He'd already seen the way her breasts could undulate within the inadequate confines of Anwuan evening wear; the thought of her running in such a state made him turn abruptly. If he looked at her any longer his body would begin to disobey, and he could not have that, not here in the dark where they were virtually alone.

"Is that a command or a request, Prince Ikem?"

There was humor in her voice, but there was a slight challenge, too. In response, Ikem turned and headed for the door. He didn't have to take this. He didn't even know why he'd said it.

"Sir!"

At that, he turned; Adama was staring at him with those enormous dark eyes, rubbing the gooseflesh that had risen on her arms.

"The little king," she whispered, casting her eye upon the baby's cot.

Ikem felt his mouth twitch upward, then, without taking his eyes off her, pulled a slim phone from his pocket, pressed a button.

"Yes, sir?" The voice that came through was crackling, yet alert.

"Two guards to the royal nursery. They can expect to be there for an hour."

The guard assented, and the line went silent. Ikem slid

the device back into the hip pocket of the joggers he wore beneath the dressing gown. They stood looking at each other, wordless, until the guard tapped discreetly. His eyes widened slightly when he saw Adama and the prince regent, but he said nothing, only took his post next to the bed. His partner was just outside the door.

"If anything happens to the child, you will answer for it," Ikem said softly.

"Understood, Your Grace."

With that settled, he turned and walked toward the door. He did not look back to see if Adama followed him until they were well away from the nursery; when he did he took in a breath. She had taken off the bonnet she wore to sleep, and the thick, soft twists in her hair brushed her strong shoulders. She'd pulled a knit sweater over her singlet but hadn't drawn it together; the lines of her body, equally strong and soft, were still very much on display. Her nipples thrust out, dusky and firm beneath the thin fabric; he had to swallow.

Ikem wanted Adama.

He wanted her badly, and he'd seen that same hazy smokiness in her eyes in other women often enough to know that if he drew near her now, she might react favorably, despite their surroundings. Perhaps she'd even welcome the chance to regain some control over the situation after being put in such a vulnerable place, back in his nephew's bedroom.

"Will you come?" he asked. His voice was low and gentler than it normally was. It was a voice that was intended to entice, not to challenge or to agitate, and Adama lifted one small hand to her head, tucking a twist behind her ear. He wanted to touch her hair; he knew from looking that it would be soft as the finest wool and frame her beautiful face like a cloud.

She felt it, too; he was sure of it, and she was walking toward him now, hips moving in the gentle sway that had occupied his thoughts at the most unsuitable times since that night she'd walked away from him in the Obelisk Courtyard. He also remembered that he'd vowed inwardly, after their run on the grounds, he'd never touch her. Yet, he was here, and so was she, and nearly all of the skin that had been covered by black Lycra was open to his gaze.

"To take a walk, or something else?" Adama said flatly, and Ikem blinked. He had not been expecting such a blunt rejoinder, but then again, this was the girl who had been introduced to him by plunging his head into the Obelisk Fountain.

"What do you think?" he asked, and he could not keep irritation from bleeding into his voice.

Instead of facing him outright, she leaned carefully against the bit of wall closest to him and tipped her chin up. Unlike her shyness in the darkness of the nursery, she did nothing to hide the proud thrust of her breasts this time; her nipples were tight and swollen. One had nearly broken the confines of the garment; he could see the dark circle of areola peeping from above the sagging neckline.

His mouth grew dry; then it watered. He'd already smelled her skin; tasting it would be—

"…fine?" she was saying, her voice husking softly through those full lips.

"Excuse me?"

"I said, is this fine, Your Grace? You seemed to like this position the last time."

The fortress that was Adama was pulsing with strength; the walls were higher. She was *mocking* him. Ikem's eyes narrowed, and his nostrils flared as he processed the challenge.

He'd always been a good scaler.

"You can't be serious," he said and laughed, then moved closer to her.

Hunter and quarry? Which was which? Her nostrils flared slightly. He knew on some level that she could unman him with a gesture, but this was about more than physical ability. "And?" He allowed his eyes to flicker over her; the way her rapid breaths made her chest rise and fall, the teeth digging into her lower lip in between words.

"I shouldn't be serious," she agreed. "But I'm an—honest person, Your Grace."

He was close enough to press against her in a way that was quickly growing familiar, similar to their encounter in the garden, though it felt as distant and hazy as a fever dream now.

"Is this wrong?"

Adama licked her lips; he had never before, he thought, seen a woman look so resentful and yet so like she wanted him. She tilted her head up so that her mouth was within easy reach of his, and it was she who closed the distance between them, lifting a hand to press against the smooth hardness of his chest, as if it was an opportunity she could not pass up.

"You're so warm," she whispered.

He bit back a groan; her touch was heady heat that engulfed rather than attacked. It was like being submerged in one of the nearly unbearably hot baths he favored; the senses were completely overwhelmed.

Gods, she hadn't even touched him yet, not really.

"I'm going to kiss you," he said, and there was barely time for her nod of assent before he lowered his mouth to hers. He'd been wild to taste her, and was not disappointed, not in the least. She was heat and sweetness, new wine, the type that slid so smoothly past your defenses you did not realize until you were thoroughly, dizzyingly drunk.

Ikem heard wood creak and realized he'd pressed her harder against the wall than he would have if he was more in control of his faculties. She was doing, it seemed, all she could to encourage the rough handling, though.

"Ah," she gasped against his mouth. "Yes—"

He felt nails dig into his back and became almost instantly, powerfully hard.

Adama's body softened beneath his as wax does on a hot day; he could feel her shifting, adjusting herself so that more of him was against her. She slid a leg between his; her thigh came in contact with the part of him that felt most sensitive at this particular moment, and he gritted his teeth against a groan. Adama could feel his arousal, surged to meet it; she gloried in it.

His eyes flickered downward.

"Do it," she said, breathless. She bit her lower lip and squirmed up, and that was enough encouragement for Ikem.

Ikem lowered his head, drew a nipple into his mouth. Even through the thin fabric he could feel it harden all the more, swell for him. His hand went instinctively to cup her other breast, stroke the hardening point with his thumb; it was heavy, warm, fit perfectly into his palm.

So sweet.

Adama made a low sound. She did not stop him; on the contrary, her fingers went down to grip the soft coils atop his head, anchoring him there. When he bit gently, she let out another sound, keening soft and tense, something that sounded like a yes. And this time, he forced his head up past her hands.

He wanted to see her face.

She was breathing hard; her eyes were wide, dark and full of desire, yes, but that desire was laced with a pain so acute he actually froze. Wordlessly, he reached out and braced his palm against the smooth softness of her cheek.

"Your Grace—" she whispered.

He was about to answer her, to tell her to come to his room, perhaps, and ease the burning in both their bodies.

But she kept talking.

"I was dreaming," she whispered, "about the day he died. My brother."

Adama's trembling voice was ice to put out fire, and Ikem stepped back, feeling as if he'd been slapped. The headiness of desire he felt was gone, replaced with—not anger at her words, per se, that would have been completely irrational, but anger at the fact that the rug had been yanked out from under him so spectacularly. There was shock—a registering of sudden vulnerability on her face. The walls were still up, but he could see cracks in them, air blowing through, cooling the heat under his skin.

In that moment he saw it all. Her nightmare. The wounds she hid, jagged and raw. The way she flinched away from him now, hiding her face as if in shame. Her fear of being seen as weak, a fear he shared on a daily basis.

Fear not of desire, but fear of uncontrolled feeling.

He'd gone too far. *He'd gone too far.*

"You—you tell me this *now*?" The words flew out before he could stop them, cold, exact, the opposite of what his aching chest wished for.

Adama blinked. "I—what?"

Ikem wiped his mouth on the back of his hand; blood

was drumming in his temples. He could still taste the sweetness of her mouth, her skin. "You did this—why? So you could accuse me of pawing a vulnerable woman like a drunk—"

"Your Grace—" Her mouth was trembling, but he hardened his heart.

"Well played, Lieutenant," he said coldly and drew his dressing gown closed. The two stared at each other for a long moment; then Adama straightened up, still more than a little unsteady. She looked positively ravished. Her lips were swollen, her hair was half-undone and there were twin circles of wetness on her breasts, where his mouth had ravaged her.

Despite his anger and her distress, he knew it was not an image he would forget any time soon, and that made him even angrier.

"In the garden the other night," he said slowly, in measured tones, "I vowed I wouldn't touch you—yes, we might as well admit it's been—happening since then. I have not kept that vow, Adama, but I assure you I will now. I pray the gods give you sound sleep, and I am truly sorry for your loss."

With that, he turned on his heel and left, his heart still beating wildly in his chest. He had no room in his life to spar with the likes of Adama Ohi. It was far too dangerous, for reasons he could not articulate, for articulating them would shatter the image of himself he'd worked so carefully to cultivate. And now—he felt little but shame. Shame at his lack of self-control.

He did not look back, although the heart that beat inside his chest longed for more than anything he'd wanted in a very long time.

CHAPTER NINE

Never in her life had Adama been so embarrassed. *Never.*

She was shaky and wild-eyed for most of the rest of the night, the sort of wild-eyed shakiness that comes from knowing one has screwed things up, and spectacularly, and of her own making…

I have to get out of here. Her repeated encounters with Ikem had proven one thing; this wasn't just about lust. If it had been, she'd have let him take her right there in the hall without a thought, professionalism be damned. They were consenting adults, weren't they? He wasn't a commanding officer. She reported to Kadir, technically, not to Ikem. And she couldn't very well claim an abuse of power when it'd been she who practically demanded he put those large, rough hands on her. She remembered the warm, wet rasp of his tongue on her nipple and bit her lip so hard she tasted blood. She could tell already that it would have been hard and heated and sticky and rough and—

But she'd fooled herself completely, hadn't she? She'd convinced herself it was *lust.* But in that moment when he was kissing her she hadn't wanted sex, or just a fling with her extremely attractive head of state. In that heated moment she'd wanted *intimacy*, and somehow instinctively knew that he could provide it.

And she'd been fighting it since that night in the garden, since that day she'd seen him recoil from Catherine Elimu as if he'd been physically slapped. Every bit of her cried out to know more about Ikem, to hear his voice, to—

She had to leave—but how? She had an assignment to fulfill.

Her only escape would be, she reasoned by morning, to catch the would-be kidnappers of the young king, bring them to justice, be duly promoted—and then, beg Kadir for an assignment that would take her far beyond the reach of the magnetic, arrogant, completely enthralling Prince Regent Ikem Eze.

When Adama returned to the nursery, she'd splashed icy water on her face until she was quite sensible again; then she sat with one of her graphing notebooks, a map of Anwu and a frown that settled deep into her brow. In the morning she was relieved by the day nurse, headed to her rooms in the barracks of the Royal Guard to wash and found Kadir.

"I need an audience with His Grace."

Kadir blinked.

"It's about the protection of the young king." *And myself*, she thought, but the gods willing, Kadir would never know of that. She'd checked with security that morning; routine camera sweeps of those very hallways had produced no evidence of their brief tryst. Either the security system was shoddier than she'd thought or Ikem had gotten there first.

The possibility made her stomach hurt.

At least Kadir hadn't seemed to guess what had transpired the night before, although she wondered if he eventually might suspect something was going on between his two former mentees. As it was, he gave her no reply except a nod and brought her to the prince after breakfast.

He looks like he's just got up off a down mattress, she thought in irritation. Ikem lounged indulgently at the massive conference table inside the throne room. He hadn't even the decency to look conflicted. She managed to clear her throat; then she took her eyes off him and focused on the other two in the room. She could not look at Kadir; he knew her too well for her to pretend all was fine. She chose instead to look at Felicité, who sat with little Adim in her lap, feeding the youngster thin slices of melon from her own plate.

"Adama," Felicité said a little impatiently. "We're all here, child. Do get on with it."

Adama bit back the first response to come to her head and cleared her throat instead.

"I think," she went on, "that the king should disappear."

At this, three sets of eyebrows climbed high; Felicité uttered a little shriek. "What?"

"Disappear," she repeated. "To an undisclosed location, for his safety. If indeed the situation is what we think it is, anyone who seeks to do the child harm will reveal themselves by coming after him. We will identify them that way."

Felicité was the first to speak, after drawing in breath that swelled her chest and letting out an outraged huff. "Use my grandson as *bait*—!"

"He will be perfectly safe, Princess. I will see to that."

Felicité drew Adim close with trembling hands. "I hate this," she whispered, her face pinched and wan, and for the first time since they'd met, Adama felt true pity for her. The woman, after all, had lost a child, a son-in-law, and now her only grandson was at risk. It was too much for any baby to have to endure, barely through his first year on earth.

Adama was silent, as were the other two men in the room. She knew that it was actually Ikem's call, his decision, but he said nothing—and in a way, she was touched by his sensitivity in affording Felicité the respect due a parent. She was the closest relative the little boy had now.

Felicité traced down the line of Adim's cheek; he gurgled indignantly. "Do what must be done," she finally said, and everyone exhaled at the same time.

"Thank you, Princess," Adama replied. "If I may take your time, I'll review the plan with all of you."

The plan was simple. Under the cover of Anwu's ink-black darkness, she and Kadir would steal away with the child, disguised as a local family, to a secure location close to the east border. Her village, in fact. And she could see what the actual situation was at the borders, although she left that bit of context out. Felicité would start a rumor within palace walls—her maids were notorious gossips—and they would see who, if anyone, came looking.

"How long will it take to get there?" Ikem asked, his first time speaking since the conversation had started.

"About two days by road, Your Grace, as we cannot travel too quickly with the baby," Adama replied. She focused on his lips instead of his eyes, which was an even bigger mistake; she instantly pictured the way they'd felt, hot and wet against her breasts mere hours before, tugging the soft points of her nipples to hardness. They'd ached so *badly*, and still did—

She resisted the urge to cross her arms.

Ikem grunted, then stood, all the majesty of the throne with him. His eyes were only on Adama, and when he spoke his words nearly made her reel.

"Your plan seems sound," he said, "barring the details, which I'm sure you'll share later. However, Kadir will not go with you."

Adama's mouth went dry; she knew instinctively what he was going to say next. "But—"

"If your object is stealth, no one will believe a bald-headed, fair-skinned Türkiyen of nearly seven feet is your husband, or the father of your child," Ikem drawled. "Aside from his marked lack of resemblance to Adim, or Anwuans in general—"

"He doesn't have to be his father!"

"He stands out too much," Ikem said dismissively. "And he'd be recognized immediately. Kadir is quite well-known, almost legendary."

"He's likely right, Adama," Kadir said, nodding. "I thought it myself."

Adama wanted to scream in frustration, but instead she bit the inside of her cheek. "What would you suggest, then?"

Kadir opened his mouth to reply, but Ikem interrupted, a gleam appearing in his eyes that quite illuminated them.

"I will go with you," he said, and he drew himself up to his full height, rising as Adama's stomach slid down to the vicinity of her toes, leaving a hollow space in her middle.

"You're just as recognizable!"

"Not when I shave." He rubbed his chin and smiled, a small smile that assured her that yes, he knew exactly how she felt and didn't care much. "I've done it before. Disguised as a simple merchant, and the father of your child. Make your arrangements, Lieutenant. We leave tomorrow."

"But—"

"It will give me an opportunity to inspect the borders, too. Quietly." His face darkened slightly then, and for a fleeting moment, a hint of genuine concern replaced the amusement—and all of a sudden, Adama understood.

It was a calculated risk, Adama knew, born of necessity. But in his eyes, she also saw an undeniable thread of something else. Something that both terrified and thrilled her.

A simple merchant, and the father of your child.

The words echoed in Adama's ears again and again, as if the blood rushing in them thrummed to their rhythm.

Ikem. In her space. Alone. With closer access to her than he'd ever had in the palace. Intensifying the proximity she'd fled from.

This was a danger greater than anything she'd dealt with before now—and later, she realized she wasn't the only one who'd noticed. Felicité brought it up in her usual blunt manner whilst folding onesies for the journey with arms that went like a windmill.

"I hope that you will not be so dismissive of your own opportunities," she said, fixing beady eyes on Adama.

"Your pardon, Princess?"

"Oh, don't play the blushing maiden. We're both women here," Felicité said briskly. "Ikem. I've seen how he stares at you, as if he'd like to pin you down to the nearest bit of floor."

"Princess!"

"What? You cannot say I'm wrong." Felicité peered at her shocked companion, then smiled in triumph. "You've noticed, too."

"I certainly have noticed nothing of the kind," Adama gasped. Her skin was so hot she instinctively pressed her palms to her cheeks. What an insufferable family!

"You haven't a mother here to tell you this, girl, but I will. Listen up. You've a very good opportunity—he's distracted now, but he's interested. If you can manage to stay out of his bed—"

"My lady!"

"—until he makes a declaration, that would be better. Encourage him, but make him work for it. The prince regent is not king, but it's one way to get everything you want."

Adama gaped at her.

"Oh, close your mouth, child," Felicité said dismissively. "The tension between the two of you is astounding. That big general of yours sees it, too, and I suspect he doesn't like it one bit—"

Adama managed—barely—to collect her wits. "Princess, I must stop you there," she said as imperiously as she could under the circumstances. "I am not interested in matrimony at the moment, and certainly not with the prince regent."

"You don't have to marry him, although why any sane woman would engage in sex without some material benefit is a mystery to me. They all become useless, in the end," Felicité finished, ominous. "Make it worth your while."

"I am leaving," Adama said rather weakly. She simply couldn't with this woman. Felicité had the gall to reach out and pat her hand in what she apparently thought was a motherly fashion.

"Have a good trip, my dear," she said sweetly, and then emotion flickered across her face unexpectedly. "Take care of my grandson for me. The gods go with you."

CHAPTER TEN

It was positively liberating, shedding the palace attire and donning the types of clothing he hadn't been able to wear in years—civilian clothing, clothing that actually looked as if it had been produced this century! Ikem canceled his meetings for the day and instead called the stylist he had on retainer, sending the woman to the shops to buy the latest in both Anwuan and global fashion.

"You're preening, you know," Kadir said dryly when he came into Ikem's chambers, watching as he held up a butter-soft cashmere sweatshirt, then put it aside for one in a slightly darker shade. "You know you're supposed to be a merchant, correct? Not Eurotrash on holiday in Istanbul."

"No one goes to Istanbul on holiday anymore," Ikem said breezily, then grinned at Kadir, who shook his head and allowed a small smile back. "Is Adama ready?"

"She's never late."

"I'm sure." Ikem yanked the sweatshirt over his head, then surveyed himself in the mirror. He looked happier than he had in years, and he did not mind showing that to Kadir, who understood him better than anyone. He felt free. Perhaps it was stupid to tempt his own resolve by setting off with Adama into the great unknown, but he'd done it, really, for two reasons: one, this mission, Adama's mission, could achieve several things at once. It would secure Adim, keep him safe. It would draw out the traitors within his own walls. And it would allow him to see, firsthand and unmasked, the truth of the situation at his borders.

And— Well…if he was truthful, it would free him, too. At least for the moment. And the thought of doing it with Adama…

He cleared his throat. "Is everything ready?"

"Yes, sir." Adama's idea had them walking out of the palace in plain sight. *"People only see what they want to see, and a not-very-grand couple with their baby will not be noticed among the thousands of tourists that visit the palace each day,"* she'd said. *"There will be a detail trailing us every step of the way, of course, and Kadir will be close at hand."*

Now Kadir sneaked Ikem through one of the palace's many inner corridors; it was a twenty-minute walk to the gift shop on the south side, the side of the sprawling edifice that was open to the public. Kadir handed Ikem the large leather duffel and backpack that held the provisions they'd need for the journey.

"There's a sedan parked out in the lot," Kadir said briskly. "Not your Camaro, but it'll get the job done. Godspeed, sir."

Ikem reached out and clasped his commander's hand. "I appreciate everything, Commander."

"I'm proud of you, sir."

"Well, you don't often get to tell a ruler that, now, do you?" Ikem's voice was dry. "I'll see you—hopefully, sooner rather than later."

He sauntered off into the bright sunlight of the early afternoon.

* * *

Ikem almost did not recognize Adama, and when he did he lifted his brows, holding back a smile. She was standing in front of a display of wooden hippos with the royal insignia carved into their broad flanks, dressed like many Anwuan housewives, in a wrap skirt of colorful fabric, sensible shoes and a long cardigan that opened over a simple cream T-shirt. The sun illuminated her radiant skin and dark hair, worn round her lovely face like a cloud. Ikem barely noticed his little nephew, who was asleep and content in a carrier on her back.

"Ikem," she said simply as he approached, and his heart skipped to hear her utter his name like that. The name was common enough among his people, so it would arouse no suspicion, but hearing it in her soft husky voice and applied to him—

"Omuma awu aru," he said, and before she could react he bent to kiss her.

Surprise tensed her frame at the endearment, but she did not pull away; in fact, she sighed a little, then kissed him back. They were kisses appropriate for a public place in Anwu; soft, closed-mouthed, chaste, but the way his blood stirred was completely disproportionate. It was as if with every touch of his mouth to her satin-soft lips, his heart swelled within his chest a little more. He kissed her in a way he hadn't kissed anyone for years, since the bloom of first love as a teenager. They were warm, gentle pecks, not tentative, but more of a question than a demand.

When they finally pulled apart, both inhaled, and Ikem was vexed to find his cheeks heating up. Adama said nothing, but her eyes were soft and very bright. Wordlessly, Ikem reached down, took her bag from her. She had a duffel much like his own, and a baby bag printed with color-ful letters of the alphabet on her other shoulder.

"We should go," she said almost shyly, and he saw her reach up and touch her lips as if she was not quite sure they were still there.

As soon as they joined the troop of tourists heading out of the palace gates on foot, Adama shifted into her trade-mark efficiency.

"It's not an easy trip," she warned. "People going to the borders usually take three days, make a vacation of it. We'll go by road first, and not all of it is good—"

"There are no bad roads in Anwu," Ikem said lazily.

"Spoken like a true king who never has to drive on them!"

Ikem smirked and steered her toward an old man with a kiosk at the side of the road, selling barbecued meat rubbed with spices on sharp skewers, fried savory cakes made of rich, mealy honey beans, fried crisp round the edges, and round donuts sprinkled with sugar, the boon of little ones everywhere. "I can't believe this old man is still here… My brother and I used to sneak out and buy from him. We'd have to beg pennies from our nannies since we never carried money."

Adama's eyes grew so round it looked as if they'd fall out of her head. "I fail to see what that has to do with—"

"Would you like one?" They were within earshot of the man now, and Ikem nodded his head in greeting. "Hail, sir. Two pieces of grilled meat for me, and perhaps cake for Adim…"

"He can't eat those yet," Adama protested.

"Why not? He's got teeth, and his grandmother's always giving him table food."

"Very good for baby, madame," interjected the old man. "I give you the soft one."

"The baby book says—"

Ikem ignored her and opened the brown leather wallet he'd had for years and almost never had a reason to use. "Two of those as well, Baba."

Adama compressed her lips. She would not, he knew, say anything until they were out of the range of the man's hearing and by that time, Ikem was halfway done with his first skewer of meat, groaning low in his throat at the explosion of spice and flavor on his tongue. "Do you want—"

"No. I do not." Adama was doing a very good impression, he thought, of one of the ruffled hens that squawked in indignation when they were caught in the rain, and he was taking a perverse pleasure from teasing her. It was simply too easy.

"Oh, that's right. Fruits and vegetables only," he drawled. "Well, I'm on vacation, and I plan to eat everything."

There was a pinched line between her brows. "We haven't got the time to eat everything, Your Grace, and this isn't a vacation—"

"Ikem." He looked down at her through half-hooded eyes. "I thoroughly enjoyed the way my name sounded on your lips before."

Adama took a sharp breath. "You must take this seriously," she implored, then paused long enough for him to toss his skewers and foil into a nearby trash can.

"I am." Impulsively, he reached out and took her hand, tugging her close enough to speak quietly, ignoring the soft gasp that escaped. "This, however, is the most fun I've had in years. I'm not ruling. I'm out in the country I love, with nothing to do but pretend I'm married to a very attractive woman—"

"Oh." At that, she retreated into herself, looking embarrassed, and he was struck, not for the first time, by the mixture of fire and shyness in her. He'd meant the tone to be light—gallant, a show that he was no longer affected by the intensity of their moments together. He swore inwardly; perhaps he'd overshot—

Then Adama matched him smirk for smirk. "Be a good father and carry the baby, then." She dumped Adim unceremoniously into his arms, then strode off with her usual determined stride, leaving him laughing.

Ikem and Adama were soon occupied with locating the unlocked car, decanting a still-sleeping Adim into the car seat, dealing with the occult mystery the buckles presented and setting forth under a sapphire sky, driving toward the border as fast as they dared, after a ten-minute argument over who would drive.

Yes, if they could keep it this way, they would be just fine, indeed.

The trip was as arduous as Adama remembered, and even harder with Adim—and his uncle—to deal with. Ikem shed even more of his princely persona the farther away they got from the palace. To her chagrin he stopped at two more food sellers, consuming the greasy snacks with relish, and when they stopped so that she could give Adim one of the premade bottles of formula in the baby bag and change his diaper with grim determination, he played with the boy in full view of the road, tossing him in the air till he screamed in delight. Ikem Eze, she decided with much irritation, was a bodyguard's nightmare.

The baby also clearly preferred Ikem to Adama, a fact

that hurt her feelings a little, although she'd never say it. She could not blow raspberries and gurgle and clap and dance as Ikem did for the little boy, although she could have watched him do so all day and never be tired. It did things to her insides, made them ache in a way that was oddly pleasurable. Still, when she tried, she froze up, felt stiff and unnatural. It was as if her twin had taken some vital part of her when he died. She was broken inside, and she didn't know how to replace what was missing, or how to fix it.

The second part of their journey would be by rail, an overnight trip that would take them deep into the heart of the mountainous regions that Anwu was famous for. They drove to the rail station, returned the sedan and walked as a family to the platform, awaiting the train. While they waited in a misty rain that had started when they arrived, Adama soothed herself by going over the next steps with Ikem, huddling beneath a massive black umbrella.

"I've arranged for a sleeper, to make it easier for the baby," she informed the prince regent, handing him his ticket and making sure Adim's was secured as well. "Once we're in there we'll be able to relax a little bit." Not that he needed to relax. He'd been treating their flight so far with all the enjoyment of a frat boy on summer vacation, and now he actually grinned at her, a smile that took the air from her lungs.

If he was heartbreakingly handsome as a prince, he was even more devastatingly so when he was so accessible. This trip was revealing things about Ikem that she never would have guessed, and the sight of him now, clean-shaven, wearing a baby on his chest with all the ease he did a crown, did things to her inside. It made her think of things she didn't even know she'd ever consider.

A husband. A family. Love, even, and at the last her cheeks grew hot at the audacity of her own thoughts. She'd always assumed she would end up like Kadir—unmarried and slightly humorless, but with the distinction of a military career. She'd never even wanted anything else after—

The sound of children playing interrupted her inner ruminations, and she looked up in time to see a group of them engaging in a game of tag, on one of the few patches of ground not occupied by concrete. The rain had created little muddy patches, and they seemed determined to get as dirty as possible.

"Jump!" their leader cried, his face bright with fun.

"Brats," Ikem muttered and rolled his eyes, patting his nephew as if he was certain the little boy would never engage in such hellionish behavior. "Where the hell are their parents?"

"I don't know," Adama replied, feeling her throat growing tight with fear, the type of fear that comes from reliving a nightmare, and in a moment she was transported to her small, skinny eleven-year-old body. She was there with them, playing on a construction site and jumping, and her brother was chasing her, his small face alive with laughter, with joy, and then, there was the sound of his feet thudding on the wood planks she'd just crossed nimbly, and a horrible, sickening crack—

"Hey—get down from there!" she yelled in a voice that did not sound quite natural, not at all. She could hear a rushing in her ears, felt cold and hot and extremely sick, all at once. She took a step forward, even though she did not quite know where she was going.

Startled by her sharp reprimand, the little boys jumped and hurried messily. It was as if the next thing happened very, very slowly; one of them missed his mark, tripped over one of the bright yellow dividers and went straight down into the shallow pit that had been marked to be filled with gravel sometime later that day.

His friends shouted, and Adama bit the inside of her mouth, hard, so hard that blood flooded it. Control would come—it always did. But it would take a moment.

She could hear Ikem laughing indulgently. He'd seen them, too, and the boy was fine; he popped right back up, much to the jeering of his mates. Some people on the platform gasped, then applauded sarcastically. Ikem looked at her as if ready to make fun of her for her reaction; then his face changed. "Adama?"

Adama shook her head hard.

"Adama." Ikem did not look amused, not anymore; there was concern on his face, she registered with cool detachment, as if the observant part of her had stepped outside of her body.

"Let's go," she said.

"You look as if you've seen a ghost."

In a way, she had, hadn't she?

CHAPTER ELEVEN

"Finish the tea," Ikem told Adama quietly, jiggling a now-sleeping Adim in his lap. He was almost drowned out by the sound of the rocking train. Thankfully, the car they were in was nearly empty.

"I made us conspicuous," she said slowly. "I'm sorry."

Ikem did not reply, just picked up the little ceramic cup of rooibos tea and handed it to her. She sipped, then grimaced and set it aside.

"You should finish it, Adama."

"I promise I'm fine." Her voice was raspy. She was seated across from him, huddled deep in her wool cardigan. Ikem wanted desperately to pull her into his arms, to hold her again and transfer his warmth to that cold body, but he could not. Something in her face was growing more forbidding with each second, and besides, Adim was beginning to squirm. He shifted in order to free the baby from his carrier.

"He could have died," Adama croaked. "The little boy—"

"He wasn't in any danger, Adama." Ikem did his best to keep his voice low and neutral, then reached into his jacket pocket for a tiny flask, silently passed it to Adama. "Drink this instead."

He half expected her to refuse, but she took it, uncorked

it and drank it straight instead—and they both winced. Army moonshine was not regulation, but Ikem tended to carry around a bit for his insomnia, or for emergencies, he supposed, like this one. Adama wrapped her arms around herself tightly and leaned back in her chair.

Not a word was said.

Ikem reached out after a moment's hesitation, touched her knee.

She flinched and drew back.

"Adama," he said gently.

She looked up; those extraordinary brown eyes were blank. She'd completely disassociated.

"Talk to me." He found himself using the same low, soothing voice he'd learned to use in the army while speaking to comrades who'd been spooked on the battlefield.

Adama's response came out in a choking, unsmiling laugh; she took another swig of the whiskey. It was a long time before she answered, and she stared out the enormous plate-glass window, watching as the train launched off from the platform with a little jerk that shifted them in their seats. Adim strained to see, and Ikem stood him up without taking his eyes off Adama.

"My brother died on a construction site," she said finally. "My twin, actually." In her lap she was squeezing his flask so tightly it had to be painful, but her face was steely. Ikem waited for her to continue, but she did not.

"I'm sorry," he said finally. All the words of diplomacy he'd learned in his years as a royal seemed to leave him, all at once; they were completely inadequate.

Adama's mouth flattened out. "We were running. I made him chase me, and some boards gave way, and he went down—" Her voice cracked, painfully, and Ikem felt his stomach twist.

"I couldn't get him out. He'd fallen too far. I should have run for help, but I couldn't move, I was too scared—"

"Adama—"

"I just stood there and screamed. People came. I screamed until he wasn't screaming anymore," she finished dully. "He was dead. It was my fault."

"Adama, it wasn't—"

He did not finish his sentence, for it was clear that Adama wasn't listening. She had retreated back into herself, back into that damned self-made fortress, covered ineffectually by skin and bone. He knew it was there, because he had nearly penetrated it; he'd felt those walls weakening more than once, then seen them go back up. He'd been *grateful* they'd gone back up.

Now, in the face of her pain, the cracks widening, he wasn't sure he wanted them to anymore. Why not pull them down completely, blow them open? "Adama—"

She lifted her chin, took another large swallow of the moonshine and handed his bottle back to him.

"Thank you," she said simply and lifted still-shaky hands to wipe at her cheeks.

"Adama—"

"I don't think talking about this will be useful, and I don't want to."

Ikem took a breath, looking keenly at her ravaged face.

"As you wish," he said after a long beat, and Adama exhaled slowly, then nodded briskly. It was almost painful to watch her; she was still so clearly distressed and embarrassed at her loss of control. "You should not be ashamed, Adama. I cannot imagine how painful—"

"I don't want to talk about it!"

He nodded. The walls were there for the breaching, if he wanted to do it. But he would not violate her in that way.

"All right, Adama," he said quietly.

He saw her shoulders relax marginally.

The two sat in silence that was only interrupted by Adim's babbling and finally, his whining. She sighed. Her slim shoulders had gone back to their usual straightness, and she looked up.

"He needs to eat, and possibly needs a diaper change," she said. "Our sleeper—"

"Yes, it's right this way. Come with me."

If she questioned Ikem suddenly taking over, she did not push it; she stood, collected her bags and followed him almost meekly, her eyes fixed on the floor.

The walk to the sleeper car was on a narrow, swaying corridor barely wide enough for one adult to pass through sideways. Adama's body ached, as well as her jaw. She'd clenched her teeth together so hard it hurt. Adim was up and very active, twisting away from her hard, straining for his uncle. Finally, the prince reached out and plucked the baby from her limp arms. Adama felt more like a failure than she had in a long time, and inside, her body still trembled from adrenaline and a vague sickish feeling that was not going away, not to mention a burning in her throat from both the moonshine and the screaming.

He'd looked at her so kindly; not with pity, but with a quiet understanding that was so much more dangerous. Pity she could snarl at. But this…

Don't you dare let him in.

She'd survived by being a fortress. If she accepted any sanctuary from the prince regent—

No.

All she wanted to do was pull off her shoes, crawl into bed and sleep for hours. They located their berth easily, and Adama lifted her chin and stepped in front of Ikem to get the door, determined to return to her former level of usefulness. Before she did so she turned abruptly and took a deep breath.

"I apologize for that display, Your Grace."

Ikem's face registered little emotion, and he jiggled Adim a bit. "There's nothing to be sorry for, Adama. Open the door."

She bit her lip, but she could not think of anything that would make things better, and unlocked the berth instead, sliding open the door. Then she stopped and stared in confusion.

As a child she had ridden in sleeper cars rather frequently on weekend trips into the capital with her parents, and was quite familiar with the spartan but comfortable accommodations. One could expect two narrow beds. A tiny washroom that managed to combine shower, commode and sink in one multilayered piece of equipment. A seat at a narrow desk, with a port for charging laptops and phones.

What she saw looked nothing like what she remembered, and she blinked. It was as if she had stepped into a miniature version of one of the finest suites at the Anwuan National Hotel. Every decoration had been chosen with comfort and style in mind, in hues of reds, brown, oranges, greens and creams found in the Anwuan landscape. The plush surfaces were not brand-new, but they were painstakingly maintained and of the highest quality.

"You'd make a better door than window," Ikem quipped and nudged Adama a bit. She moved forward without knowing she did it.

This car was a lounge car, featuring a small table set invitingly with fine traditional red-clay pottery. She could already smell the heady sweetness of rooibos tea, brewed the Anwuan way, steeping in sweet and flavorful spices, and yeast cakes were piled up on a three-tier porcelain serving tower. Heavy curtains were drawn tight over the windows, their rich color a warm contrast with the red tints of the cam-wood paneling.

"Sit," Ikem ordered and crossed in front of her in order to place Adim carefully in a playpen already set up with stacking cups and a soft blanket. The baby made a bee-line for the stacking cups, gurgling with delight, and Ikem looked at Adama and smiled, thoroughly satisfied.

"The royal coach," he said and crossed the room to another door. "Bedroom and washroom are in the next car."

Feeling completely lost, Adama trailed after him, not knowing what else to do. "How did it get here?" she asked stupidly.

"I had Kadir arrange it." His face took on a slightly arrogant tilt. "There's no way in hell I'm spending two days in a standard sleeper. You're not the only one who can plan things."

"The idea is to go incognito!" Adama cried.

"We are, Adama." Despite her distress, her name on his tongue made her shiver, and it had nothing to do with her sodden clothing, or with the events of that afternoon. "On the outside, royal cars look very much like normal ones— and this one looks like a freight. It's specifically arranged that way for discreet or covert travel. When you see it come through the capital it's rigged out to look much fancier and is attached to the Royal Locomotive. We're being pulled by a standard diesel train. Unfortunately, we'll have to take care of ourselves as palace porters would have been a dead giveaway, but I've arranged someone to come and serve us tonight as well."

"What if they give you up, or leak information?" Adama demanded.

He smirked. "They won't. The man's wife is at the palace for a…holiday that won't end until we're all back. Don't worry, she is exceedingly comfortable, more a guest than anything else."

Adama felt her blood run cold at the implication behind his casual words. She'd seen Kadir be ruthless, of course, but so far everything she knew about the prince regent had rendered the man rather harmless in her head. She did not feel fear when she looked at him, but she did feel the stomach-churning uncertainty that comes when you've underestimated someone. "Your Grace—"

"It was my wish, Adama." His tone was final, and Adama held her tongue.

Adim's presence served as a buffer to the tension she felt every single time she looked at Ikem, stood too close to him, or spoke to him. The air between them was charged and they both felt it; it fairly crackled. The little boy was excited at his new surroundings and demanded to be put down one minute, then cried to be up in his uncle's lap the next.

The first hour of their journey was spent on refreshment and rest. Rain-sodden clothing was exchanged for dry, and shoes were exchanged for soft, shapeless slippers of the finest wool, already in the suite. In the washroom Adama unpinned the two soft braids on either side of her head, then redid them and looked at herself hard in the mirror. She was still a little chilly and tired from the shock of that afternoon, and the bone-white tub looked incredibly inviting. However, there was no way she was going to sit naked in the bathroom with Ikem only a few meters away, singing in a thin, rusty baritone to Adim. It was a very silly song about a tortoise who took a wife, then became pregnant after eating witch-charmed food meant for her; she felt her mouth curve up for the first time since the train platform.

She pushed open the door to the washroom and crept into the bedroom. Ikem had spread the plush coverlet on the bed onto the floor, where he held Adim's pudgy hands. The boy was laughing.

He'd never looked less princely, Adama thought, swallowing hard, or more attractive.

He looked at her and his eyes were warm. "Did you enjoy our song?"

"You left out the verse about him dying."

"Don't you think it's too morbid for one so young?" Ikem said dryly.

Against her better judgment Adama crouched down next to them, easing herself to the floor. She did not know what caused the impulse; it was very unlike her, but something about the presence of the prince and the baby seemed to be unlocking things in her that had been dormant for years. "That's the lesson in the story, though," she said after a beat, and found herself, of all things, smiling. "My mother never censored any of it."

"Is she very moralistic, your mother?"

"Incredibly so," Adama said sardonically.

"I can tell."

"How so, Your Grace?"

He lifted his shoulders. "Kadir assured me from the beginning that you were a woman of integrity. I would not put my nephew into the hands of simply anyone, and since you've arrived I have seen you serve him with the utmost compassion and devotion. I am…grateful, Lieutenant."

There it was again, that warm flicker that had nothing to do with lust and everything to do with affection. Adama's heart began to drum against her chest. The prince regent's dark eyes had dropped almost lazily down to her lips, and she was grateful, so grateful, that she had Adim there. He was a small but effective chaperone, and a marvelous reason to deny the way her body hummed in such close proximity to his. The military had given very little time to pursue any sort of romance, and Adama had never wanted it—not until now, when what he wanted from her was written in those dark eyes.

"It was my duty," she said after a beat.

"Shall I add singing the last stanza to your list of responsibilities?" he added sarcastically. "I wasn't gifted with song."

Adama laughed out loud, the sound surprising even her, and Ikem echoed the smile, his own bright.

"I will have to decline," she said a little primly and leaned back.

"I knew you would." His tone was rueful. "It was worth it, Lieutenant, to see you smile. You barely have since we left."

At that observation Adama felt heat sweep her face, and she groped blindly for the gurgling child. She did not know what it was about him that made the stoic soldier in her react like an untried schoolgirl, but there it was. He was a prince, however. There was more chance of her flying than engaging in—

Engaging in *what*? A liaison? That would be easy enough, she supposed, her body beginning to throb at the memory of his fingers, tracing lightly over where she'd been so sensitive. She'd nearly come just from those brief caresses. It was no stretch of the imagination to think he'd be an exceptional lover. No, that wasn't the issue, either.

She wasn't just attracted to Ikem; she *liked* him. And that in and of itself was incredibly problematic.

Adama decided in a flash that—well, she'd just be honest. And if that didn't scare him off, she didn't know what would.

"I'm worried about our indiscretions," she said softly. There was something about their close quarters that screamed for intimacy, and not just the sexual kind—that would never happen, she was determined.

Ikem's eyes grew dark and stormy. "We broke no rules."

"That's not what I was afraid of."

"Ah." He was quiet, and— Well, he looked embarrassed now, looked down at his hands.

Adim yawned and pressed his small, sweet-smelling head into her shoulder; she hoisted herself to her feet, feeling her muscles strain.

Is this what mothers did all the time? No wonder they constantly looked so distracted, so wrung out.

Ikem stood as well, that odd look still on his face. She cleared her throat. "I think I need to feed him."

Ikem nodded briskly. "Sit," he said, indicating an armchair next to the double bed. "I'll go and get his food." In minutes he returned with one of the ready-to-serve bottles of formula, handed it to her. Adim saw his uncle, strained for him.

"He doesn't like me," Adama said dismally.

"He just doesn't know you well enough yet. He prefers Felicité to me, so this is remarkably good for my ego. Show the boy his food and he'll settle down."

Adama bit her lip and guided the rubber nipple to his mouth, and Ikem was right; Adim seized the bottle and began to suck greedily, if sleepily. "You know so much about tending babies."

"Not really. He is king, so we spend a lot of time together," Ikem said dryly. "Sometimes he sleeps nicely in his pram, sometimes he plays, sometimes he wants to be held. We keep things quite informal for that reason, and— Well, the baby nurse cannot be privy to every state conversation, and Felicité is not always available."

What an odd environment for a boy to grow up in, not yet able to talk, or to express his own preferences over whether he wanted to be present or not. "Poor little fellow," Adama said softly and touched his cheek. "You have no idea, have you?"

"He has *me*," Ikem said fiercely, and suddenly, hopelessly, Adama liked him very much indeed. How could she not?

"Yes, he does," she said, tilting her head. Ikem lowered himself to the bed, extended his long legs.

"I lost my parents," he said finally, "but I do have fond memories of them. I don't want Adim to feel like he's missing out on anything. If it means I have to change the occasional diaper, or have him in a sling during court appearances…he is *mine*. He has no one else but Felicité, and she is old. I will guard the Crown for him, the way his father would have wanted, and when he is of age…"

The air between them grew heavy with silence. Adim had finally succumbed to sleep, eased by the warm milk in his tummy. The swaying of the train had him sleeping deeply; he made no sound other than little milky exhalations in his sleep.

Adama broke the silence. "What will you do then?"

"Do when?"

"When the king is of age." Adama stood and crossed to

the cot at the end of the double bed, passing close to Ikem in their close quarters as she did so. Could she feel the heat actually radiating from his body, or was that simply the imagination of an overtired, fevered mind? She bent, laid the baby down and straightened up. When she turned she had to bite her lip against the roiling in her stomach; the intensity in Ikem's gaze was too much.

"No one has ever asked me that before," he said slowly.

Adama swallowed. "I mean no offense, Your Grace."

"I know." There was a slight frown on his handsome face. "I had not thought that far, not yet… There once was a time when what I wanted seemed possible, but not anymore. I have to protect my brother's legacy. I have to protect Adim. When he is twenty-one, I will be—" his voice trailed off "—closer to sixty than one would like."

"Is ruling so different from what you wanted to do?"

He smiled, but the gesture did not reach his eyes. "Does not everyone want to rule?"

"I wouldn't. It sounds dreadful," she said decidedly.

He laughed out loud and looked at her as if he'd underestimated her, or missed something he hadn't thought to look for before. "Are you so concerned for my happiness, then, Adama?" he asked.

There it was—that reaction she'd been having since that first night they'd sparred together, flame burning on naked skin. Adama felt as if every cell in her body was growing tight with a tension that was now all too familiar, as if they were being gripped in a vise, one from which she needed release. She clapped her hands to her cheeks. She had gone too far—not because she'd annoyed him, but because she'd started something she wasn't sure she could finish.

"I'm sorry, I did not mean—" she whispered. "I meant

no disrespect," she finally said through lips that barely moved.

"You're nosier than Kadir made you sound," he growled.

She shook her head as if to clear it, then moved to go around him. "It's warm in here."

He laughed at that. "It's not warm. You're embarrassed."

Yes, she was, and panicked, too. She hated enclosed spaces, hated not having a form of escape. The walls seemed to be closing in, like they must have done with her twin. She'd often tortured herself, thinking about what his last moments must have been like, choking on air polluted with debris, in pain, waiting for help that would come too late…

She could see the prince's face change as the room began to spin. "Adama—"

"I feel faint," she whispered, and then Ikem took two steps forward. His arms were wrapping round her, drawing her close to lean against the massive rock wall that was his chest. She could smell sweat from the day's journey and the finest oils, oils that would make his skin soft and gleaming beneath his traveling clothes. The attraction was there, yes; her treacherous body still ached for him, fitted perfectly against his own. There was more, though, something she could not as easily articulate. She wanted comfort, and yes, it was coming from the oddest place, but it felt more real than anything she'd experienced so far today, or perhaps ever.

Allowing someone to comfort her was completely new, and as frightening as it was strange, but she could not have resisted it any more than a moth could resist flame.

"I'm sorry, Your Grace," she said, but she did not move. She hated the vulnerability of this stance, but she quite honestly feared for her feet. She concentrated all her efforts on not crying—she'd humiliated herself quite enough today.

"Adama—"

"You did well, sir." Her voice was fierce with conviction, then broke on the final sentence. "You have done *far* more for your brother than I was able to do for mine."

CHAPTER TWELVE

THE RHYTHMIC SWAYING of the train, combined with the sleeping tea Ikem gave Adama after their simple dinner of vegetables and bean stew, had the desired effect, and she was asleep, still fully dressed, curled up in the middle of the double bed in the royal bedchamber. *His* bed.

After he was sure she was asleep, he drew up the armchair and settled himself into it—ostensibly to ensure Adim did not disturb her, but in his heart he knew better. There was a tightness in his chest as he looked down at her sweet, sleeping face. The pain that had been there earlier had been smoothed by rest, but she flinched occasionally, as if the tea she'd taken could not completely overcome the demons she fought, even in her sleep.

Guilt weighed heavy on her slender shoulders; that much was obvious. She wouldn't have been the only one to treat internal pain by a stint in the army, and she would not be the last. He reckoned that Kadir himself had his own damage, and what better than a life of service and routine to take one's mind off one's own struggles?

After all, it had worked for him, when he had been young and angry and resentful of his place as the royal spare. Now he'd gotten exactly what he wanted—to be as important as his brother, but the price was one he'd pay for the rest of his life.

Adama shifted and made a soft sound in her sleep; Ikem shifted as well, more uncomfortable inside than any stiff upholstery could make him. He could not want Adama, not in any capacity; sometimes he thought that wanting led to curses, that the gods mocked him even as he wished.

He would much rather do his duty and never be disappointed—or disappoint. And by the gods, it would be easy to disappoint Adama, though his body and his mind both felt inexplicably drawn to her. Were there no restraint, were he to follow his instincts, he'd take her in his arms, hold her close to his heart, tell her that everything would be fine, that she would eventually heal, be happy again.

He might even manage it without sounding like the hypocrite he was.

As if in response to his thoughts, Adama's eyes fluttered, then opened. She was fighting sleep with all her might, and despite the seriousness of the situation he smiled to see it.

"Adim," she whispered. "Some bodyguard I am…"

"Consider yourself relieved of your duties for the night."

Adama sighed and stretched, shifting into a more comfortable position. Her soft, full breasts thrust outward and he immediately focused on her forehead. He would not look. Not when she was like this.

"I am so very sorry," she murmured, closing her eyes, and he was not sure whether that apology was for him, or for herself.

"Adama…"

"It's cold…"

It was not cold, not at all, but Ikem stood, his throat constricting. He took the coverlet from where it was draped at the foot of the bed and pulled it over her, up to her neck; she exhaled again, soft and sweet, lifted a hand up and touched his cheek. It was barely a touch but it warmed him, all the way to his toes, then back up to his head. He tried to tug back, but she did not loosen her grip, soft as it was.

"You're very kind," she mouthed, barely audible, and he felt his chest turn over so violently he thought he'd be sick.

So much for his resolution. *Business, indeed!*

This was very, very bad.

When Ikem woke the next morning, sore from his night in the armchair, he could see slivers of light from the outside, filtering in through cracks in the curtains. Adim was propped up in his cot, babbling and clapping along to a song playing on a tablet situated just high enough for him not to reach. Adama was standing with her back to him, arranging dishes on a tray with her small hands. Gone was the skirt of yesterday; instead, she wore tight jeans and a black sweater that hugged the small of her back, basically a variation of her Special Forces uniform.

When she turned there was no hint of the vulnerability that had characterized her movements the night before; her face was stoic as ever, harder, if that were possible. "Good morning, Your Grace."

He didn't want this shift to formality, even though it was decidedly more comfortable than anything else last night might have led to. "Adama," he said shortly.

She did not complain at the informality. "We will arrive by evening, sir, and then take a smaller train into Eleku. Mother will be thrilled to host you."

"Why am I filled with uncertainty at that?" he murmured and stood.

Adama's eyes skimmed his chest and darted right back

up to his face. He remembered belatedly that he'd shucked his shirt sometime in the night, tucked it under his head, too lazy to get up and fetch a pillow from the other room. Self-consciously, he dragged a hand over the bare skin there, although part of him felt pleased she'd noticed. It was the sort of pleasure he hadn't felt since he was a young man fresh from university, flirting with girls at court.

"I will lay the table," she said softly and practically fled the room, the baby in her arms.

Thank the gods, Adama thought for what felt like the thousandth time that morning, for the baby. She wielded him like a shield, used him as a certainty that nothing would happen between herself and the prince. The child's proximity made it easy to avoid the muscled, sinuous heat that was Ikem Eze, to ignore the fact that every time he drew close, her body's reaction, unexpected as it was unwelcome, was completely out of her control. And after yesterday, she did not trust herself. Not even a little.

They dared to open the curtains just a fraction, since the train was at high speed, and it was unlikely anyone would be able to glance in the windows to see the splendor within, and watery sunshine spilled onto their table, illuminating the hot cereal in pools of cream, the strong tea, the fresh fruit. Adama balanced Adim on her lap and fed him slivers of fruit, as she often saw his grandmother doing; the little boy ate them eagerly. Ikem raised his coffee cup to her in mock salute.

"The boy is really enjoying himself."

Adama smiled, a small one that flitted across her face; Ikem raised his brows. "And that's one of three times I've seen you smile since we headed out here."

His assessment made heat rush up again. "Have you been counting?"

"I have."

She cleared her throat. Embarrassment fought with irritation, and the first emotion won in a landslide. "This is not a business that fosters smiling."

"Kadir smiles…sometimes."

"That's because his salary is obscene."

Ikem's laughter rang out, and Adama was warmed by it. She liked the way it reached his eyes, made them crinkle at the corners, and felt her body relax…slightly.

"You'll be up for a raise after this trip, that much is certain," Ikem said, taking her bread from her hands and buttering it for her when she struggled with the baby. He placed it back on her plate with a portion of rich, creamy-white cheese. "What is our movement today?" Unlike the night before, he now seemed content to follow her lead.

"We switch trains in the afternoon, and we reach our destination sometime in the middle of the night." She hesitated. "We will then go to my family home. It's near campus and quite private."

"And stay there until…"

"Until the perpetrators expose themselves."

"Very well."

Adama shifted. "Mother lives a rather quiet life," she said. "She's very discreet. Also—she has a business, a boardinghouse of sorts, that's been taking in refugees. It'll be a good way of hearing what's really going on."

Ikem's face was quiet, but there was something in his expression that was hard to read. "And your father?"

Adama swallowed. "They're no longer together." Their son hadn't survived, and their marriage hadn't, either. She'd felt guilt for years over her role in taking her parents' marriage as well as their son. It had eased as she became a woman and a soldier, but it still resurfaced at the oddest times.

"Oh, I'm sorry. Recently?"

Why was Ikem so adept at pushing the tenderest places, prodding the exact spots where it would hurt the most? *You checked up on me. Why don't you tell me?* she wanted to spit out. But instead, she said what was in her heart.

"It's hard on a marriage to lose a child." That horrid choking was building in her throat again; she cleared it and took a long sip of the near-scalding tea before she felt able to speak again. "I wasn't much help," she admitted. "I grew up to be quite an angry teenager…the military saved me, in a way."

He nodded as if he understood. "Be cheered, Adama," he said, simply. "You've done well."

CHAPTER THIRTEEN

The next leg of their journey took place in the cramped general sitting area of a small local train, filled mainly with mothers and children, workers heading home after their shift and many, many college students, gossiping and flirting, singing along to the pop music playing tinnily over the speakers. Ikem, face half-hidden by the hood of his sweater and a wool cap, watched them all with bright-eyed curiosity and an odd half hunger in his eyes.

What she didn't like was the fact that he now treated her with the gentle consideration that one would a child, or someone who was ill—someone *fragile*. It grated on her nerves, a soft, insistent erosion of the discipline she'd built brick by painful brick. She hated herself for exposing herself to Ikem so fully, and she blamed exhaustion and the stress of the past few weeks for her misstep. Ikem now knew about the death of her brother and her reasons for joining the military; what he didn't know, however, was the breakdown that had followed and how hard it'd been to overcome it. Kadir had made sure she saw a therapist within days of joining the army, and she'd managed to channel that pain into being the greatest soldier she could be and rising to unprecedented levels in their ranks.

In a mere day and a half, Ikem had managed to shatter

everything she'd taken years to build, and she was terrified of it. Of him. She sensed that there were depths beneath the steely surface she had yet to explore, and instead of wanting to flee, she was drawn to them. To him.

What she needed to do now, she thought, was ensure that the prince regent understood that she was fine, that she didn't need him anymore, that she'd never needed him.

You don't need anybody. She repeated the mantra to herself, jiggling the baby on her lap.

"Adama, are you all right?"

She blinked, looked up at Ikem. He must have been staring at her for quite some time; concern had furrowed his brows, and she bit back a curse. She'd keep that woebegone look off her face if it killed her. "Yes," she said, biting off the *sir* just in time, remembering that she was supposed to be talking to her husband, the father of her child. As if reading her thoughts he reached out and drew her close to his side, indicating the window. "We're almost there—see the river?"

She looked in the direction he indicated, but she couldn't see anything. Adama smelled the spice of the oils he used, mixing pleasantly with damp Anwuan wool, cashmere from the finest of the goats that roamed the hills in the North. She stiffened involuntarily and remembered just in time that she was supposed to like this. A twinkle in his eye when he looked down showed he was thinking precisely the same thing.

"Wishing you could drown me?" he said dryly.

Adama shocked herself when laughter bubbled from her lips. Adim looked startled, then laughed uproariously himself, clapping his chubby hands. An older lady across the aisle with a basket in her lap passed Adama a golden, fragrant pear and smiled indulgently.

"So sweet." She spoke in Eleku dialect, in those soft drawn consonants, and to Adama's surprise Ikem answered in the same language. His vowels, rounded by frequent trips abroad and boarding schools, were completely disguised; he sounded like any of the boys she'd grown up with.

"I'm a lucky man," Ikem responded and bent low so that his mouth hovered close to hers. "Am I not, Adama?"

He's going to kiss me, Adama thought, and it made her blood run hot with want and cold with panic. She expected him to claim her mouth with his own immediately, but he did not—and the question in his eyes, and how it was rendered, was perhaps what made Adama sigh and part her lips.

Ikem's kiss, as was his touch, was far different from what she expected; it was gentle, considerate, asking rather than demanding. His kiss made her feel as if he could have pinned her down and ravaged her mouth if he wanted to, but he'd chosen not to, and that made all the difference in the world. When he pulled back a moment later he left her with a body that cried out for more.

She ignored the good-natured chuckle of the old woman, and Ikem's answer—something about them being new parents, going to visit her mother—and buried her face in Adim's clean-smelling neck, focusing on the scents of talc, shea butter, sweet-smelling oil. She could feel the gaze of the prince as palpably as if he were touching her; they had unfinished tension to resolve, tension that had sparked in those first few heady moments when they'd discovered that they were so equally matched.

"Adama."

She swallowed and forced herself to look up. Ikem was smiling, his white teeth sinking deep into the flesh of the pear, and his tongue darting out to touch his lower lip, chasing the sweetness of the juice.

Adama swallowed. That was doing nothing for the trajectory of her thoughts and she suspected Ikem knew it. She wished she had no idea what his lips, what his hands, felt like.

"What?"

He lifted his brows mischievously. "She says that Adim looks like you. Finally, someone thinks so."

She permitted herself a small smile, then occupied herself with Adim while Ikem and the woman gossiped. When the train stopped he helped the older lady carry her bags to the platform and was rewarded with an enthusiastic smack on his cheek and two more pears from her basket. He turned back to Adama, who was wrestling with the straps of Adim's carrier.

"Let me take him," he said casually, reaching out for it, but Adama took a full step back.

"No need," she said tartly. "I'm fine." She had to be fine, had to prove to Ikem that the events of the past twenty-four hours meant nothing, were just a blip. She was a soldier, and a good one, not a shivering girl who cried over things that had happened over a decade ago. She wanted some separation between herself and Ikem as well. They had exited the train at least twenty minutes ago, but she still felt his warmth against her skin as much as if she were still sitting there, nestled into that hollow in his side, a hollow that seemed custom-made to fit her body.

I need to stop this, and soon.

Wearily, she led Ikem to what would be the last leg of their journey—a bus, owned by the campus, that would take them close to their final destination: her family home.

Hopefully, her mother wouldn't pass out when her only

daughter showed up unexpectedly with a man—and a baby. Once inside the bus she lifted Adim to her shoulder and fixed her eyes on Ikem. He was quiet, looking out the window at the fading sky.

"Ikem," she said quietly, her voice sticking a little on the word. Without the formality of his titles, the address felt curiously intimate.

"Adama," he mocked, looking back at her. "What are you thinking about? If you frowned any more that glass might melt."

She swallowed, hard. Ikem's large, warm fingers trailed down to find where her free hand lay limply in her lap; he took it between his and squeezed gently.

"You're doing marvelously," was all he said, and the emotion that bubbled up in her chest was enough to make her panic, open her mouth.

"You can't do this," she whispered.

His brows lifted. "Do—"

"You know exactly what you're doing." Her words were short, jerking. "Being all—kind and charming. It's a terrible idea, and we won't be here forever—"

He glanced around furtively for a moment, but he needn't have worried. The passengers who weren't wearing earbuds were chatting among themselves; there were no sweet old ladies, not in this bus. "Adama. I certainly did not —"

"You kissed me."

His eyes gleamed, obsidian-dark. "You kissed me back."

Breath rushed from her lungs. "I—"

He looked round, then leaned in, cupped her face with his large, warm hand. "Sweet Adama," he said in the dialect of her region, and she felt that heat in her face turn molten, trickle down to her chest, her arms, her legs, all the way down to her fingertips.

"You made a mistake, letting me out of the palace walls," he said quietly.

"I didn't let you out. You insisted on coming!"

He smiled at that. "True." His thumb ran down the length of her cheekbone, then over her lower lip, and Adama's heart beat wildly. Surely, he would not try to kiss her here, like this—but gods, his fingers were skimming the bare skin at her collarbone now, and she could feel her breath trapped close in her lungs, feel her body begin to arch toward his, almost helplessly.

"There," he said quietly and bent to kiss her neck, just a whisper of contact on a spot already left bare by her sweater. Stubble scratched her skin. This was wildly inappropriate, in the midst of such a public place, but her body was in direct opposition to her head.

"This is hopeless," Adama whispered.

"I know," he said back just as quietly. "It's—been there since the night you nearly had me burst my lungs, trying to keep up with you in that damned garden—"

"Your Grace—"

He let that settle for a long moment, then leaned in again, kissed the shell of her ear with lips that were both slow and hot. Adama felt the quiver deep in her nether regions; it spread in waves, lightning-hot to her breasts, making her skin tingle. He laughed without smiling; sadness flickered across his face.

"Play-acting," he said. "Remember? While we have the freedom," he said, "enjoy it with me, Adama."

Something had shifted. Something that rose in her throat made her mouth dry. And she was powerless to stop it.

CHAPTER FOURTEEN

THE BUS COUGHED to a halt, scattering chickens and a couple of goats. Adama lifted Adim to her shoulder, feeling the small, trusting weight of him.

Her shield, Ikem had called the little boy in jest. And he was growing more ineffective by the moment.

Ikem, beside her, stretched, the wool of his sweater taut across his broad shoulders. He looked every inch the merchant he pretended to be, although his posture did nothing to dim the latent power that she knew hummed beneath his skin. He scanned the familiar landscape, the peak of the Ceres Mountains a darker smudge against the fading sky.

Home.

"We're here," she said, her voice a little rougher than she intended. She hadn't expected to feel such emotion in the pit of her gut.

"It's beautiful."

From the bus depot, they took a hired car the rest of the way, Adama pointing out landmarks as they went—the university, the school she'd attended growing up, her mother's squat youth hostel close to the center of town. Her family home was a bit on the outskirts; it rose out of the side of the mountain, a large stone house that seemed to have sprung fully formed from the earth.

A garden crawling with wild Anwuan roses and trees heavy with summer fruit surrounded the property; Adama could smell the sharp wincey apples, fragrant, fleshy mangoes, and her stomach growled.

As they stepped out of the taxi, however, a new scent joined the familiar ones of home. There was a faint, acrid tang of woodsmoke, masking a more subtle aroma that hinted of many bodies in close quarters. Her family property, while large, usually echoed with quiet. Today voices rose and fell in the wind—unfamiliar, accented voices.

Then, Adama saw them.

Tucked discreetly behind a row of tall plantain trees, near the disused barn her grandfather had built, were makeshift shelters. Tarpaulins stretched over salvaged wood; blankets hung as doors. Small fires smoldered, thin plumes of smoke rising lazily into the twilight. Figures moved amongst them—women stirring pots over flames, children huddled together, men sitting, faces etched with weariness.

Refugees.

Beside her, Ikem went still.

Surprisingly, it was Adama's mother, not Adama, who kept Ikem from breaking down completely.

It was worse than the reports. Much worse. The intelligence—it had been filtered. Sanitized. Adama's mother took him round, introduced him to people who had been there for weeks. The *stories* he heard—

He did not know what to expect from Adama's mother, and so he had no expectations. She was a neatly dressed woman, looking much as her daughter did, but with softer edges and an intelligent light in her eyes. She wore her hair in a similar style to Adama's, braided and twisted in loops that covered her ears, shot through with threads of silver and white. In an instant Ikem could see that she was a woman who had been through much; she registered no real surprise or curiosity at the sight of him, and he'd worn a medical mask over the lower part of his face, giving a cold as an excuse for his disguise. She gave them a tour of the grounds with brisk efficiency and answered Ikem's many questions about the refugee situation with clarity and eloquence.

She was working with the municipality, as were other people with extensive grounds, she explained. Their property served as temporary shelter for refugees as they were documented and checked, then rehoused in more permanent places there and in nearby villages—mostly hotels, hostels and schools that were out for the term.

"Who is this?" she asked, her eyes widening when she saw the baby, and her worn face lit up in a way that made it just as beautiful as her daughter's. She took the young king on her lap, only half listening as Adama explained that Ikem was a friend from the army, and this was his son.

"The child's mother is no longer with us," Adama said smoothly, glancing at Ikem without a hint of nervousness, and her mother's face changed.

"I am so sorry," she said, reaching over the table to pat Ikem on the back of the hand.

"Don't be. She's not dead. She just left me," he said dryly.

Adama's mother inhaled at that, but her breeding was as good as Ikem's—she asked no further questions, and when he asked for space to make some calls, Ikem was ushered to guest rooms as fine in quality as any he was used to back home. He drew back the finely woven linen curtains on an enormous plate-glass window that looked out on the distant peaks, arching above lush greenery and blue water, and despite himself he felt his throat fill with an emotion he barely indulged in the capital.

Anwu, he thought, was beautiful. Heart-achingly beautiful, all of it, and this glimpse of it, from the windows of the woman who'd served it as faithfully as he tried to do, affected him more than it ever had within the shrinking walls of the Sun Palace. He pressed a hand to his heart.

Catherine was right. And now he stood here, beyond humbled, pricking beginning at the corners of his eyes, as emotional as any old soldier on the country's National Day.

Anwu. The Sun. Small, but great.

He picked up his mobile and dialed. The call didn't take long, not at all.

Not long after he'd finished speaking there was a tentative knock at the door of the bedchamber, and Ikem gulped hard, then straightened up, steadied himself. "What!"

"It's Adama," came a voice from the other side of the door, and before he could formulate an excuse for why she should not come in, the handle turned and the door opened.

When Adama saw Ikem, his huge shoulders filling the frame of the window, her mouth went dry despite herself. He'd crossed his arms over his chest in an absolutely forbidding manner, but the emotion on his face…

"What is it?" he demanded, then turned to the window, his back to her.

"I brought you towels." Her mother's maid, Oby, was occupied with the baby. Her mother had sparked to life in a way she hadn't seen her do since her father had left the family home; she immediately ordered her staff to go to storage, produce the cradle and playpen and toys that Adama had used as a child. Her mother's penchant for never throwing anything away had become an asset in this case, she supposed, and she was currently in the process of turning her sewing room into a makeshift nursery. She hadn't even let Adama touch Adim, and the little boy was thrilled with his new caretaker, snubbing Adama unapologetically when she'd tried to take him back.

"Take some towels and sheets to your friend. I need Oby to help me with the baby," her mother snapped, eager to have her daughter out of her way. "You know, Adama, you can't always be useless with children."

Adama had just shaken her head and left. She could hear her mother at her back, singing an old lullaby to Adim in a thin, reedy soprano that the little boy tried his best to match with yowls and babbles. Now she stood barefoot in the entryway of the room that had been given to Ikem, with an armful of snowy towels that smelled of lavender and black vanilla.

"Oh." His voice was reluctant to concede its confrontational tone. "Thank you."

Adama crossed the floor silently, taking a moment to run her hands over the softness of the duvet, heavy with traditional Anwuan embroidery round the edges. There was something absolutely forbidding about Ikem's stance, something radiating from him that was so dangerously intense, she was afraid to draw closer.

"Dinner is at six," she said lightly. "Let me help you with those windows. The rooms are kept clean, but they aren't aired as often as they should be." She tugged her sleeves over her fists, crossed the room and came up beside him. "Prince Ikem?"

He did look at her then, and the mixture of emotions on his face startled her, as did the hint of wetness on his lashes. Something had affected him, standing here, and greatly. She saw the muscles work in his throat as he swallowed; then he spoke, his voice low and nonchalant, but still strained.

"It is Prince Ikem again, is it?"

She felt heat rise to her cheeks; it did not even surprise her anymore as that seemed to be her body's reaction to him all the time. "We are alone, sir."

The words lingered in the air much more suggestively than she'd intended, and she took a step back. Ikem paid her no mind; he was still gazing out on the landscape before him, smoke tendrils curling upward toward the sky from grills and cooking fires. "I called Catherine," he said abruptly. "Sanctions—it'll be official in a day."

She nodded, a lump rising in her throat. "You did the right thing."

"I did the *only* thing," he corrected. His voice was laced with anger—not at her, but at himself. Then he cleared his throat.

"I owe both you and your mother more thanks than I can ever say."

Adama shook her head. "I live for service to the Crown, Ikem."

He ignored this. "Your home—it's beautiful. I appreciate your mother's opening it up for this purpose."

Adama tugged nervously at a braid. "They built it when we were little, before..." She paused.

"Before your brother died," he said quietly.

She cleared her throat. "Yes. They wanted to sell it, at first, but quickly saw how foolhardy that would be. It's tripled in value since then."

Ikem's eyes, still holding that recently acquired shock and sadness, kept darting toward the window, toward the distant, faint plumes of smoke from the makeshift shelters.

He ran a hand over his ink-dark hair, a gesture of deep agitation Adama hadn't seen since his private torment after the Catherine meeting.

He was no longer the detached prince, nor the confident merchant. He was simply a man grappling with a truth he hadn't allowed himself to see.

"It's worse than the reports," he murmured, his voice rough. "The sheer number." He turned so his back was to her; she suspected he didn't want her to see his face. "My brother's policies were meant to ensure stability. Alliances. His *marriage*, even—"

"Sir—"

"They were miserable, my brother and sister-in-law." Ikem was speaking slowly. Deliberately. "Did you know that? Every rumor you probably heard was true and more. I think she married him only to escape her father, but she didn't find herself in a much better situation with Adim the Second. They didn't last two years. And then he died—"

His voice trailed to a natural end, and Adama remained standing at his elbow. There was an odd mix of fear and pride stirring within her; it had been easy to deny herself the man with the title, but the Ikem who now stood before her was so very different.

"I am ashamed," he said, and his voice was almost too low to hear. "My utter—pride, my self-centeredness—"

"You wanted to uphold his legacy, Your Grace. It was admirable, in a sense."

"I insisted on upholding a legacy I didn't understand!" He turned to her, eyes dark with anger. The analytical mind, the soldier's precision, seemed to reengage, but it was now overlaid with something raw and fierce. "I saw the numbers, but I didn't *see*." He stopped abruptly, looking at her. "You saw it. You knew. Or at least, you suspected."

Adama met his gaze despite the tension still licking through her body. "I am from this region, Your Grace. My family has lived here for generations—but even I knew nothing until my mother told me. We've both been isolating ourselves."

A muscle worked in Ikem's jaw. And when their eyes met this time, Adama felt no nervousness, no reticence. Only a sense of shared purpose.

"I'll need a landline, if you have it," he said simply. "A computer, too."

She nodded. "We brought secure lines and modems with us, sir."

"All right. Let's get to work. Catherine and the Parliament will handle the sanctions—the gods know she's had them ready for weeks. You and I can work with Kadir on aid for here and the rest of the border towns—and as long as we're here, we can oversee it."

"Yes, Your Grace."

CHAPTER FIFTEEN

THE LANDLINE WAS finally silent, the secure modem powered down.

The weight of the day settled in the quiet study of Adama's childhood home, now the site of something she knew would one day be called a major historical event. It surprised Adama, how quickly Ikem's mind worked, and how he came to conclusions with near-mathematical accuracy. Kadir, his voice slightly distorted over the line, began sending out the necessary orders. Ikem spoke to Catherine as well, sent his digital seal and signature over to her, and watched as the announcement of the sanctions was made live on social media, on television, on radio. Ikem was seeing the kingdom, and his role in it, with new eyes. And now—

Ikem stood at the window, not looking at the mountains, but at the faint, distant glow of campfires, flickers in the dark. Adama came to stand beside him, leaving a space between them.

Adama could hear his unspoken thoughts as clearly as if he'd shouted them to the rafters. "Sir."

He made a noise low in his throat.

"You did more for them in three hours than anyone has in three months," she said softly.

He didn't turn. "It's not enough." His voice was rough with self-recrimination.

"It's a start," Adama insisted. She reached out, her fingers hesitating before resting on his forearm; the muscle underneath the soft wool flinched. "Ikem. Look at me."

He finally did; the hollowness Adama saw in his expression took her back to that day in his chambers with Catherine, when fear of incompetence had been stalking him like an evil spirit.

"You were a son trying to honor his brother," she corrected gently. "Now you are acting as a true king."

Ikem covered her hand with his, his thumb stroking her skin. The simple touch drew the line between them taut, knotting it tightly. She couldn't have drawn away even if she wanted to, and God knew she didn't want to.

The bleakness outside was real, but here, in this quiet moment, something else was real, too.

Hope, mostly. And an intensity of feeling that it'd be foolish to deny.

Ikem brought her hand to his lips, kissing her knuckles; she closed her eyes, took a deep, cleansing breath, registered the softness of his mouth.

"I've never had such an effective partner since I became regent," he said simply, and the compliment suited her better than any she'd ever received, warming her to the tips of her fingers, taking the last of her defenses with it. "Thank you, Adama."

They'd worked so hard. And they'd worked as if they'd been doing this together for years.

Something flashed across Ikem's face, a memory that gave him pause.

"Adama, where's the king?"

Adama started. She'd completely forgotten about Adim. "Why—he's still with my mother, of course."

"He technically was supposed to be here for all of this," Ikem said wearily, rubbing his eyes with the back of his hand. "Damn it."

"I won't tell if you won't," Adama said dryly; and they both exchanged a conspiratorial smile. It seemed rather silly now, the pomp and circumstance of court, after what they'd seen today. Ikem had really stepped into his own as a leader today—he was owning now, no longer maintaining. And here, shrouded in the warm shadows of this guest chamber—

"We should take our rest." He dropped her hand. There was something in his voice that she was afraid to prod at, to try to decipher. It hinted at something that made her body tighten with memory. And by this point she knew it wasn't just lust. She licked lips that suddenly tingled, as if they remembered what had been and were adjusting themselves for more.

Stop it.

"Your mother's divested you of your shield." Amusement colored the vowels of his voice again. "It's been days since I've seen you without that boy dangling off your neck."

"I'm at home," Adama said, trying to keep her voice light, and Ikem's eyes flickered over her, unencumbered by the work that had kept them so occupied all afternoon. She was wearing one of the many outfits she'd left at home before leaving for the army ten years ago: a white V-neck T-shirt, so thin from washing that her skin gleamed through, lounge palazzo trousers of the softest cashmere. She'd rebraided her hair, placed a touch of gloss on her lips. Now she wished she'd added a sweater. She did not have to look down to know her nipples had overcome the thin bra she wore beneath her shirt and were jutting out, dark and full.

Swollen with anticipation, or desire, or a combination of both.

Part of her wildly wanted to laugh. Why the hell was she fighting this, any of it? She'd wanted Ikem since the moment she'd set eyes on him, and though she'd taken the position with absolutely no intention of becoming his mistress…

"You look amused," Ikem observed.

"I *am* amused."

"Why is that?"

"Beginning of the month, I was getting ready to take my leave, and the most exciting prospect I had was a trip to Lagos to see a cousin. Now—" she shook her dark head "—the Prince Regent of Anwu is in my childhood home. He knows my whole story, and I know his. And I'm in his bedroom because—" She could not finish that statement; she cut it off. Ikem's eyes began to gleam.

"You're in his bedroom because of what?"

Gods. He wasn't going to make her ask, was he? She could feel her skin burning as if he'd touched her already, feel the blush spreading vivid-hot over her body. She knew what these sensations meant; she wasn't ignorant.

Specifically, she wanted the prince. Those slow, large hands and warm lips…she pressed her lips, and her thighs, together. Perhaps if she— Perhaps if they pursued this, it would slake the fire that had been burning low and steady. It would be over, and then they could both finally move on.

Ikem looked at her for a long while before walking, steady and slow, over to the door; she closed her eyes, heard rather than saw the bolt being drawn. When the tread of his footsteps was close to her she let her eyes flutter open. He was looking down at her, an odd expression on his face.

"The lock on the door doesn't bother you?" he asked.

She frowned, confused. "What?"

"The lock." Ikem cleared his throat. "I've noticed. Whenever we're anywhere enclosed, you gauge the exits right away."

Of course he'd notice that. "Special Forces training," she said quietly. "And… I don't like the idea of being trapped. Here it's fine, though. This is my home."

"Right." He reached out almost hesitantly, placed his hands on her waist, as if he didn't know what to do with them, or if he was—nervous, if that were at all possible. She could feel the warmth of his skin even through the shirt, and it took her a full moment to still the trembling that threatened to overcome her.

It was just so much.

"What does this mean?" she found herself asking.

"It means," Ikem said, his voice growing rough, "that I'm going to try my best to go slowly, and you'll tell me if you want me to stop."

Her face grew hot at his boldness, but courage found her, and she closed the distance between them with a step, rose to her toes, kissed him hard on the mouth.

Enough of this timidity, this hesitance! She was a warrior, from one of the finest families in Anwu. She would not be defeated by her own fears, or be stilled by over-analyzing this. It was simple; her body throbbed for the prince, and she would have him. She hoped he'd be quick, passionate, *rough*. Yes, that would do it—beat back all this noise in her head—

There was a moment, and then—

Why isn't he moving?

"Ikem," she whispered, the question raw. "You know that we can't do this if it's going to be— This can't go beyond this."

He looked genuinely confused, lifted one heavy brow. "You think that's possible, Adama? After all of this?"

"I think you're a king," she countered.

"Regent."

She ignored that. "And I'm a soldier. And yes—I want you, but it would be in both our best interests if we—have no reason to be—"

"Intimate?"

Adama took a deep breath. "Sex isn't intimacy."

"No," Ikem confirmed, and his mouth tipped up slightly. He reached out, cupped her cheek in the heat of his hand and she couldn't help but close her eyes.

"Don't you see how well you *fit*, Adama?" Ikem said gently. "In everything, not just in this?"

Adama was aware that Ikem wasn't moving, and yet, he was closer still. She'd been closing the distance between them, almost involuntarily. All she knew was that if he didn't take her in his arms she'd die from the want that was cramping her body.

That was the most frightening thing of all.

"You know—" he murmured, and he was even closer now, deliciously close, all heat and spice and warm, sweet skin. When her lips brushed his jaw he hissed a little but kept speaking. "I thought of you as a bit of a fortress, Adama. But in the past few weeks I've seen a few glimpses of the person inside. I'd never force myself in, but I—" He stopped to collect himself, to measure his words. "I understand why you guard her, really I do, I'm like that myself. But I'd like a little more of you. I can't help it. You're enchanting, my love."

His last words were the quietest yet, heavy with something very close to regret, to reluctance, and they landed with a force that surpassed any physical blow she'd ever been given. With them went the last of her composure. Emotion rose, hot and fast and unfamiliar, and a single tear escaped and traced a hot path down her cheek. She didn't wipe it away. He couldn't see it, anyway; they were pressed together now, the hardness of his body adjusting to fit hers, cradling her close.

"Adama..."

"You know what happened to me," she whispered against his neck, a poor attempt to answer the question she saw burning in his eyes. He didn't know what he was asking her for. If she—did this, if she opened up to him, she'd be surrendering. Not her body, or even her mind, but the wound she'd been hunched over all these years, protecting it.

"Adama—"

"I stopped speaking," she murmured, the confession stolen from a place she kept locked away. "After he died. For a year. If I hadn't found the army—you don't understand how bad feeling hurts, Ikem. It's not that I don't want to. But—"

"Adama, look at me."

She lifted her chin unwillingly; Ikem's gaze was searching. It'd shifted completely from desire to something less superficial, something deep and aching. "I know what happened to you," he said, his voice rough with an emotion that she recognized. "And I know what it is to be haunted by a brother."

Haunted.

Trapped.

Adama closed her eyes, but his voice pushed past her feeble attempt to shut him out, to protect the last bit of her armor.

"You think you're the only one with walls?" he continued, gently thumbing at the dampness on her cheek. "Every decision I've made as regent… It's been a question." His voice was smooth, hypnotic, almost. "What would he have done? I've been trying to rule as his ghost, Adama." He exhaled. "I've been so afraid of tarnishing his legacy that I almost forgot to have one of my own."

Adama heard the things he hadn't said, as audibly as if he'd continued. Guilt. Inadequacy. Things she wrestled with every day. And his lips tilted upward. "We've both been quite the performers, haven't we?"

She stared at him as if seeing him for the first time; the pull of desire had dissolved, replaced with something nobler, something sweeter.

Truth for truth. Pain for pain.

A wound for a wound.

He leaned in, and when his mouth met hers, and his hands slid beneath her shirt to burn the skin of her back, she sighed.

It wasn't a kiss of seduction; it didn't have the sear of mere passion. Not anymore. This was a kiss that held a promise that in this room, perhaps—just perhaps—they could lay down their ghosts, if just for one night.

CHAPTER SIXTEEN

THE WARM, WET SLIDE of Ikem's tongue on hers made Adama startle—pleasantly, yes, but still startle. She was not aggressive, but she was eager, and Ikem kissed with a quiet assurance that stirred something in her; she flowered to life beneath his touch.

Kissing was quickly not enough, and the little sounds of pleasure that hummed deep in Adama's throat urged him on to more.

Her body, she thought, must be next, and it was as if he read her mind. Adama gasped as his hands found her breasts, weighted them hot and heavy in his hands. His fingers knew what to do instinctively; gentle passes of his thumbs over her hard nipples as he kneaded gently, pausing to kiss her in between those soft breasts.

"Adama," he said, and his voice was a low growl this time, wrapping possessively round her name, as if he owned it, owned her and had no intent on letting her go. She opened her mouth to speak but whimpered instead as he tugged her turgid nipple between thumb and forefinger. Her head dropped back slowly, and he took the opportunity to bend, press a featherlight kiss to the column of her throat.

Then he took a step back, dropped his arms to his sides

and his lips curved up into a smile that was absolutely heartbreaking.

"Touch me," he said, and his voice was gentle. "Wherever you'd like."

If Adama's skin was any hotter, she thought, she'd incinerate on the spot, be reduced to a pile of ashes. She did not know where to look, or what to do; she stood immobile in the spot he'd left her in.

Touch me. Wherever you'd like.

By the gods, she wanted to. She took a hesitant step forward, then did what he'd done to her, slid her hands beneath the hem of the shirt he wore. His muscles tensed as her hands slid over them, and so did his breath. As a soldier she'd seen more than her fair share of men, both clothed and unclothed. She'd had lovers before. But this sort of exploration...

Ikem grunted softly when she tugged, and he helped her yank the material over his head. Her mouth grew dry at the sight of him; he was all corded muscle and smooth dark skin, peppered with little marks here and there.

"Touch me," he said again, and the sound he made when the flat of her hand skimmed his abdomen—

She saw muscle work beneath the smooth skin and knew he was holding himself very, very still.

Working completely on impulse, Adama's fingers skittered across the hard, smooth line of his hip, down to where hard muscle disappeared into the waistband of his trousers. She dared not go any farther, and she suspected he knew it; there was a glint of something very much like amusement in his eyes. She lifted her chin in response and took the plunge, thrusting her hand down and gripping him, velvet hard and silken warmth, in her hand.

He did make a sound then, and Adama felt satisfaction

that was tempered only by lust. Her tongue darted out, small and pink, and it was time for Ikem to lift his chin.

"Touch me," he repeated, hoarsely this time, and Adama stroked him only once before he swore loudly, swept her up and kissed her the way she suspected he'd intended to all this time, thrusting, invading her mouth with a sweet roughness that only heightened the tension racking her body in two.

"I tried to be patient," he groaned against her lips, and she laughed. The unfettered joy of the sound surprised her more than anything.

'And *I* told you to be rough."

Ikem did not waste his time; his large callused hand was rough against her skin, yet still so gentle she twisted for more. Too gentle; it was sweet and torturous and she supposed he knew it. He cupped her first through the butter-soft fabric of her trousers, and even through that—

"There, Adama, you're so wet."

At that, a moan broke from her throat, both breathy and reluctant. His fingers slid against her folds, still impaired by the soft cashmere, and she instinctively spread her legs, and spread them wide, because she wanted more, and he wasn't giving her— He was yet to touch her there, but it already felt so *good*—

"You must let me take these off first," he said dryly, voice cutting through her haze of lust, and her face grew hot.

"Do it, then," she snapped, and his voice rumbled low in her ear as his fingers hooked her waistband, tugged downward. She fairly trembled with anticipation; nothing in her imagination could have prepared her for the want that drew every muscle in her body tight. She held her breath till she was on the bed, and he was drawing her shirt over her head.

He looked down, silent, at where she was wet and aching, until her body hummed with heat, and everything pooled down to that single, throbbing place between her thighs. She wanted him to touch her so badly she shook, but she would not ask. Not today.

Ikem bent close to her, so close that the chain round his neck brushed the skin between her breasts. Her thighs did not need much coaxing to spread for him, and he ran his fingers gently down over her navel, her mound, all the way to where the skin was pink and swollen and glistening, framed by smooth thighs. He parted her, and she took a breath. "Ikem—"

"Wider," was all he said, and she felt warm breath against the most sensitive parts of her.

Yes, damn it, yes—

Just as she tensed for the contact he was up and kissing her, stroking her face, her hair, her breasts. Her nipples were hard, near-painful nubs of sensation at this point, and each brush of his fingers sent a slow wave of pleasure that coiled round her spine, burst warm through her abdomen. There were streaks of warm wetness on her thighs, on the sheets; it did not take much time before she let out a little whimper of frustration, pushed his dark head down.

Ikem laughed quietly as he acquiesced, and his lips seemed to sear her skin, pausing at her navel, going lower. There were leisurely swipes with his tongue, gentle nips with his teeth. He rested his head on her inner thigh, lazily parted her folds, traced a finger back and forth along her labia. It did not take long for her to thrust her hips forward, swearing at him, and he laughed and finally, finally lowered his mouth to her.

Adama stiffened in pleasure.

Gods, his mouth was so hot. Hot and wet. His lips were so soft she could barely stand it, but the stubble on his chin grated against her like fine sandpaper. It was very hard to keep still, and the bastard was not quite there and he knew it. She angled her hips then, bucking wantonly into his mouth, twisting, trying to get him to—

Adama moaned long and loud when he finally found the little swollen bud. He teased her expertly, starting with long liquid strokes followed by quick little flicks, always pulling away at just the vital moment.

How the hell did he *know*?

She thought she heard a chuckle when she swore again, and she found his ear and pinched as hard as she could to punish him. Of course he lifted his head then, looked into her eyes and smiled.

"Ikem," she gasped.

"Adama," he said gently and mounted the bed himself. He slid one finger into her and then another when she gasped, turned them.

"Ikem—"

"Is this what you want?"

She nodded, and when his thumb finally skimmed over her clit something sparked, leaving her nerves raw, exposed. She didn't know how much she could take, but he rode her spasms with his fingers. A well-placed thumb had her finally crying out, clenching against him until the energy was drained from her, and she sagged back weakly, trying to remember who this woman was in real life.

Ikem's eyes fairly blazed at this point; she felt as if she were someone else, reaching up to thread her arms round his neck, pull him down to her. It was the only way she could communicate what she wanted; her voice had left her throat.

"I have no way of protecting you, Adama," he said, low, and she was confused for a moment; then she understood.

Oh. Her cheeks colored, but she reached up, threaded her fingers through the chain on his neck. She tugged until he hissed.

"I am protected," she said softly. "My injection—" She did not continue. Ikem, as a member of the military, would know what she meant; it was standard for active female soldiers. "Please." She could feel him bumping up against her entrance, and her body surged for him again. She wanted this.

Adama was realistic; they likely had no future, but for once she would put her wants before everything else.

"*Please*, Ikem," she said and reinforced her statement by reaching down and touching him through the fine cloth of his trousers. He hissed, then tugged them down, and Adama closed her eyes.

"Stay in my room tonight," Ikem whispered.

Or at least that was what she thought he whispered. She lay naked on his chest, skin to skin, still throbbing with the warmth that had been him, pulsing inside her. There was a vague stickiness between her legs and her heart was so full she could not move or raise her head for fear that it would all spill over.

Now Ikem's hand was warm, caressing her back, down to her bottom, over her hips. His touch was imprinted on her skin; she wondered wildly how women lost themselves so completely over their lovers, and the answer came to her in a rush.

This felt this way because of the emotion that fueled

it. The act of sex itself had been merely a result of what had been brimming in her since she'd met him, and she'd thrown herself over to him completely after mere weeks' acquaintance.

Her employer. And the current regent.

This was by far the most foolish thing she'd ever done, and she found she did not care.

He sighed so deep that she rose and fell with his chest, and his other hand slid up to join the one tracing gentle circles on her skin. "Are you all right?"

She nodded into his neck; she didn't trust her voice. She could feel that softened part of him twitch against her leg and her throat grew tight; her body hummed with awareness. She couldn't possibly—

She cleared her throat. Behind them, over his shoulder, she could see the clock; it was late. They'd missed supper, and supper meant they would have to leave this little cocoon they'd created for themselves, locked in the prince's room.

"I should go," she said quietly.

In response, Ikem flipped her over in one quick motion that her brain remembered was from Special Forces training, pinned her to the bed, his eyes dark with amusement. "Finished with me so soon?"

She laughed in surprise, a breathless sound that broke from her unexpectedly. "Mother will expect us soon. And I really should check on Adim…"

Both pithy excuses, and both of them knew it. Adim was likely happier than he'd ever been in his life with his new playmate, and her mother with her new houseguest. Also, she thought a little darkly, her mother would be delighted, knowing her reticent daughter had finally taken a lover. "I'm an awful bodyguard."

"You were hired to protect him during official engagements," Ikem countered. His eyes had grown smoky with lust, fixated on her breasts, which stood out full and proud from the wall of her chest. He uttered an oath, reached down to cover them with his hands, then leaned down to nip at where they spilled over. Adama's breath caught in her throat. Her breasts had always been rather sensitive; in Ikem's hands they felt so *good*. He traced round her nipples with his fingers till she squirmed; he knew exactly what she wanted and he wasn't touching her like that. It wasn't fair.

"Ikem—" she gasped.

"Yes?" He rolled her right nipple between his fingers as he bent down to scrape gentle teeth against the other, sending lightning-hot messages down to that bundle of nerves between her thighs, that sweet secret place that Ikem had discovered. She was paralyzed with how good it felt; she could not speak except to gasp out his name.

"Your body is delightful," he said against her skin. He was teasing them to hard, almost painful points, dropping his mouth down to kiss her stomach, breathing warm air atop her mound. She didn't want him there—she was far too sticky, and to both her relief and frustration he stopped short of parting her folds and stood to his feet instead.

Dizzy from arousal, Adama blinked. He was there as well, thickening and lengthening before her eyes.

"I'll be back," he said a little huskily and disappeared into the washroom.

In an instant he was there again, bending between her legs. She felt the steam first before she did the heat, and he was gently cleansing himself from her thighs. The warmth felt heavenly on her tender sex, and when he was done he dropped the towel on the floor, scooted in close.

Adama felt oddly sad. Ikem knowing exactly what to do spoke of lovers past, and she didn't want to think of that in relation to him, though she had no business being possessive. She'd known him for such little time. And if she thought about how reckless, how *stupid*, she was being, lying here, letting him take her in the smoking ruins of the fortress she'd maintained for so long—

Instead, she turned so she could press her breasts against the wall of his chest and dropped her hands down to touch him. She could feel him jerk, swell in her hands. "Adama—"

"I want to," she insisted, and as she said it, she could hear her own voice thickening with lust.

His voice was a low chuckle deep in his chest. "Rougher this time, then?"

"Yes," she said flippantly, glad for the lighter tone, though her heart was thudding so loudly she wondered if he could hear it.

CHAPTER SEVENTEEN

ADAMA WOKE TO the insistent press of sun-warmed linen against her cheek. For a long moment, she lay still, utterly sated, her body humming with a deep, liquid warmth that had little to do with the morning light.

She was naked, tangled in sheets that smelled of jasmine and spice and…

Ikem.

The memory of his mouth, his hands, the delicious weight of him, thrummed through her, making her toes curl. This was a new kind of pleasure, so potent it felt like a dangerous indulgence. Her own voice, thick with uninhibited sounds she barely recognized, echoed in her mind. She, the disciplined soldier, had become—

Then, the warmth began to curdle, replaced by a cold dread that seeped into her bones. Her carefully constructed fortress, years in the making, had not merely been breached; it was now dust. Every lesson, every hard-won piece of self-control, had dissolved in Ikem's bed.

And now Adama had to catalog the damage.

It wasn't the sex. That was manageable.

The damage was in the gentleness in his voice when he'd spoken of his brother, the feel of his forehead against hers, the way he'd tilted her chin up, looked into her eyes as she'd tightened with pleasure at the way he filled her, and she shattered in his arms. She had done more than share her body; she had shared what hurt her most.

Adama shifted and froze; the rustle of the sheets was like a shout in the quiet room. Ikem stirred beside her. He rolled onto his back, stretching, the lean planes of his torso rippling under the soft glow of early morning. He looked utterly content, a lazy, sensual tilt to his full mouth.

A pang, sharp and unexpected, twisted in her gut.

He turned his head; his eyes were dark and heavy-lidded with sleep. "Good morning, Lieutenant."

The intimacy of the address, the possessive warmth in his gaze—

It hadn't been just sex. If she'd managed to delude herself in the heat of the moment she would not do so now. How the *hell* could Ikem be so calm, when she felt like a raw nerve, exposed and screaming? She felt the ghost of her twin's hand, still warm, slick with blood, and the primal terror of that day surged high up in her throat. She could not, *would not*, risk this kind of shattering again.

"Your Grace," she managed, her voice a reedy whisper. She clutched the sheet to her chest, creating a flimsy shield between them.

His smile faltered, a flicker of something she couldn't quite decipher—concern? Confusion?—clouding his eyes. He reached out, his large hand brushing her cheek, his thumb stroking gently just beneath her eye. "Adama? What is it?"

She flinched.

"It…" Was a mistake. *A catastrophic, beautiful mistake.*

"We can't do this again," she said, the words torn from her throat, tasting of ash. She scrambled back, away from his touch, until her bare shoulders pressed against the cool stone of the wall. "We…we were reckless."

He sat up; the soft look of early morning gave way to something harder. "You say that, Adama, but your eyes tell a different story." He paused, his gaze dropping to her mouth, then flickering slowly over her, a caress that set her skin tingling. "You cannot deny what passed between us. I will not permit it."

"You will…*not…permit*?" Adama said slowly. A flush, hot and unwelcome, spread across her cheeks. She hated this, hated the way he could strip away her composure with a look, a word. And she lifted her own chin, leveled her gaze to meet his. The anger and indignation was welcome; it would steady her. "It was…a moment of weakness. Of exhaustion. We are soldiers, Prince Ikem. We know how to compartmentalize. How to move *on*."

"Move on?" His voice hardened, a flicker of that familiar princely arrogance returning. "Is that what you call it? You speak as if it was a fleeting encounter in a barracks, not—" He gestured vaguely, encompassing not just the bed with its rumpled sheets but the shared vulnerability of the past days. "You felt it as keenly as I did. And you're a shitty liar, Adama."

Her breath hitched, and the pressure in her chest became unbearable, mingling with a rage that bubbled up—not at him, but at the entire situation. Ikem was pushing, pushing at the very core of her defenses, the walls she'd spent years fortifying. *No*— She swallowed hard. "I'm a fantastic liar. You just can't take the truth, like most men—"

Ikem crossed the bed in a flash, held her wrists with his long fingers. His face was furious. "I think you forget that you owe me a sparring match, Lieutenant. Let's not start it now."

Adama jerked backward; the errant sheet slid away, and in one breathless moment they were skin to skin, her breasts crushed against the hard wall of his chest. "You're hurting me!"

"You and I both know you could have me on my back on that floor in less than a minute, Adama. If you're going to do this—you're not going to be a coward about it. Tell me."

"Is that an order, sir?" she taunted.

Ikem inhaled sharply; he released her immediately, regret clouding his face. "It's—" She saw the swallow he took work its way down the column of his throat.

They were both quiet for a long moment; Adama felt the anger leech from her, and Ikem's shoulders drooped as well.

"I cannot," she began, her voice cracking. "I cannot have this." She fought to regain control, to articulate the terrifying truth. "You are everything I ran from."

He frowned, closing the distance between them, and reached out as if to cup her face, but she flinched away. "What do you mean?"

Well—he wanted honesty, and he'd get it. She couldn't stop it even if she wanted to; the words were tumbling from her mouth.

"The responsibility," she whispered, her voice barely audible, thick with a pain she rarely allowed to surface. "The weight. The expectations. You… You'd demand everything." Her vision blurred. "You wouldn't mean to, but you would."

"Adama—"

"I watched my brother *die*, Ikem. I heard his screams grow weaker and weaker until he was gone. I had to go home and listen to my parents tell everyone what happened, again and again. I ruined their lives, their marriage—"

"Adama, it was an accident!"

"Ikem, I don't have anything to give you. I wish I did, but I don't. Not anymore." Her cheeks were wet; she swiped angrily at them. "And sex isn't going to be enough for you, and you deserve more than that. I cannot lose myself, Ikem. Not in you, not in anyone else. That part of me doesn't—work. Not anymore."

She saw the immediate impact in his eyes; a flash of recognition.

He understood. Possibly more than she would allow herself to think.

"Adama," he said, his voice impossibly gentle, reaching for her again, his touch like a balm she desperately craved but still fiercely resisted. "You won't lose yourself with me. I would never ask you to break. I…"

You wouldn't mean to, but you would.

Seconds ticked by, hanging heavy in the air; Ikem's eyes hadn't left her face. He'd pull on the princely mask any moment now, Adama thought, and misery was cold at her chest.

"Adama—" he began.

He was interrupted by frantic banging at the door; Adama drew the sheet tight round her as he yanked on his sweats, made his way there as fast as he could. He could hear Adim babbling on the other end of the door.

He opened the door, just a crack; Adama's mother was there. When she saw his maskless face, she took a full step back, her own growing slack.

"So it's true," she whispered. "Your Grace—"

Shit. Adama began to get off the bed, then remembered

she couldn't—her *mother* was there, for God's sake. She closed her eyes. Her head was beginning to pound.

"Your men are here, sir."

Kadir and his conclave of men had arrived with great fanfare, a helicopter landing, directly in the open field adjacent to Adama's mother's orchard. Ikem and Adama dressed silently, then left the room swiftly and met them in the study downstairs. There was no time. No time to talk, no time to decide on a cover story for why she was in his room first thing in the morning, no time to address the fact that she'd said—

We can't do this again.

She was right, of course. And he should be grateful they had been given such a quick and easy exit. But still—

Ikem forced his mind to the task at hand. Duty first. His heart, such as he had one, would have to wait. Everything had to wait for the Crown.

"Sir?"

Kadir's had been a dramatic arrival, a stark contrast to Adama and Ikem's clandestine journey. Kadir was grim-faced and regal in his dress uniform and followed by a detachment of loyal guards; Adama's mother seemed quite in awe of him. The poor woman had received the shock of her lifetime, probably. Baby Adim, wide-eyed in the older woman's arms, watched the spectacle.

"Commander," Ikem said, his voice flat.

Kadir didn't waste time. "Your Grace," he began, his voice hoarse, "the mission was a success, sir. Queen Consort Sabine—"

Anger tensed his body even at the mention of his former sister-in-law. "She's no queen of ours!"

"Spies associated with Sabine were apprehended on

the route here yesterday. They have confessed. Her intent was to kidnap King Adim and use him to destabilize the Crown, to force a change in leadership. She believed you, Your Grace, were too—" he hesitated here "—distracted."

Ikem's face did not move, although he knew it must be a study. Sabine. *Of course.*

"Is Felicité in on it?" he asked through lips that felt numb.

"She claims innocence."

Ikem closed his eyes briefly. The lack of sleep and the disruptions of the past two days were making his head pound. If he could just have a moment, a quiet moment to process this—

There was a soft exhalation of breath, then, from Adama, and he opened his eyes again to see every single one of his men on one knee, fists on chests, head lowered.

His brow furrowed.

Kadir, the only one still standing, produced a slim wooden box of iroko wood. Ikem recognized it instantly. Adama must have, too; hence the gasp.

"Adama, come here and hold this," Kadir said. "Then kneel."

Even before Kadir said a word, Ikem felt his heart begin to beat oddly, felt a hot flush begin somewhere round his chest, rising up, the choking of premonition. No. *No.*

"Princess Sabine's confession revealed more, Prince Ikem," Kadir continued, his voice ringing with a newfound formality, the voice of a herald. "The records, the lineage, everything points to a deliberate deception by the former king's wife, a betrayal of the bloodline."

He paused to let the words sink in before continuing. "There is no one left in the direct line except for you."

Then he knelt as well. His head tilted low. "Hail to His

Majesty the King," he declared, his voice cutting through the stunned silence. "Ruler of Anwu and all its territories, Keeper of the Sacred Trust, Conduit of the Ancient Mysteries…"

Adama gasped. Her mother, beside her, made a choked sound, then lowered herself, balancing the baby as she did so. Adim, oblivious, clapped his chubby hands. The world tilted, the air around them suddenly thin and sharp. Somewhere in the middle of it Ikem heard his voice emerge as if from a stranger. "Kadir—what the hell is this?"

Kadir stood. Ikem couldn't decipher any emotion on his face save for his usual professionalism, that soldier's demeanor he wore like a cloak. "You are the rightful King of Anwu, Your Majesty. And I have brought you the crown."

The world seemed to spin faster then. The sounds of the forest, the distant bleating of sheep, the murmur of the stream—all faded. Only Ikem's rigid stillness remained. He looked at the box, then at Kadir, then his gaze, haunted and lost, found Adama's.

She turned away.

Ikem reached out as if propelled by an unseen force and plucked the diadem from the box.

Aside from Adim's laughter, the whole room was silent. Ikem again tried to lock eyes with Adama, who refused to meet them, and kept them trained on the floor. And he knew instinctively that whatever walls had crumbled beneath them the night before had been rebuilt, and with double thickness.

CHAPTER EIGHTEEN

Ikem would return to the capital three days later with all the full regalia of the kings that had come before him. Kadir, in keeping with his nature, hadn't left out a thing. The royal helicopter was waiting, now perched precariously on a neighbor's flat rooftop, and he had clothing from Ikem's wardrobe, in appropriately royal colors. Ikem slipped on the bracelet and signet ring used for court appearances, but refused the diadem. His stomach hurt every time he looked at it.

"Not wearing it doesn't change anything," Kadir pointed out.

Ikem glared at him. "If it's all the same, then, I'll wait."

There was some conversation on what to do with the displaced king, who spent much of the afternoon crawling into places the adults were too distracted to keep him from. He was finally popped into a playpen, complaints ignored, and plied with toys and teething biscuits until he was quiet.

"Technically," Kadir said gently, "he is no longer your responsibility. His grandmother—"

"Do you expect her to tend to him while being investigated? Don't be foolish, Kadir." Ikem spoke more sharply than he intended, showing the tension that had been roiling through him since Kadir had appeared.

I have brought you the crown.

Ikem squeezed his eyes shut. The diadem was not on his head, not yet, but he could already feel the weight of it, pressing hard, making his temples ache. Overpowering. He remembered laughing in the mountains with his unit in the pale watery light of the dawn, passing around a canteen of illicit gin, easy comradeship and glorious anonymity. He remembered traveling with Adama on the mountain train, holding her close, kissing her as if he had no other responsibility but to take her home, cuddle the baby in their care, make love to her, eat and sleep.

Their time together already felt dreamlike, shrouded in the same mists that clung to the mountain peaks in the morning. They'd both known this time was coming, but now that it was here—

And she hadn't come to him. Not once, though he'd left his door ajar each of the three nights. She hadn't even looked at him, not really.

When he was dressed and ready to go, Ikem came into the sitting room to say his goodbyes. Adama's mother was all nervousness and excitement; the revelation that she had been hosting the king was a shock he supposed she'd never get over. Kadir elected to stay with the helicopter, and Adama was—

"I'll leave you two alone," her mother said, looking from one to the other and back again, then backing out of the room.

Ikem looked down at where Adim was, struggling to get free; Adama held him fast. Her shield was back, he thought with a rueful smile, and in more ways than one. She looked at him warily, said nothing.

"You're the best of friends now," he said, gesturing to Adim.

The corners of Adama's mouth turned up, just a little. "He's a good boy." She hesitated for the briefest of moments. "Did you have any idea? About his—parentage, I mean?"

"While they were together?" He shook his head. "My brother's wife seemed faithful, although now I have a feeling that their marriage was more as a result of Felicité's ambitions than hers. Kadir suspects one of her bodyguards that she'd brought from home."

He did not miss Adama's wince.

"What happens now?" he asked after a beat.

"I'm not going to quit, if that's what you're thinking," Adama said stonily.

He felt his gut tightening and fought the feeling down with all he had. He could not, could *not* afford to be worried about Adama, not with what he had in front of him. And yet, even at this moment, she was all he could think about.

"I'm sorry," he said simply.

She flinched and held Adim a little tighter. "Sorry for what? We knew this had no future."

"We never *discussed* it!" They'd made love—*once*, for the sake of the gods. And then—then she'd said—

"Still…" She lifted her shoulders once. "We are both practical people, Ikem."

How could she be so indifferent, after all they'd shared? "Adama—"

"I'm not going to fall apart over this, if that's what you were expecting," Adama said. "Go home, Ikem. I will follow. I will join the Guard, and I will serve the Crown as I've always done."

Ikem's jaw tightened. The words she spoke were as prudent as they were true; they were words that he likely would have said himself in her position. They were alike, he and Adama, and loved their duty too much to keep it up. He could not be selfish, not when so many depended on him.

Adama, as was her wont, said nothing. He wondered fleetingly what it must have been like for her, that year when it had been too painful for her to speak. He'd never asked her. There were so many things that he'd wanted to ask her, but there hadn't been time. They'd gone from friends to lovers in mere days, and now they were back to being ruler and subject, with walls erected higher than ever.

He cleared his throat. "I don't want you to worry, Adama," he said. "You have nothing to fear from me once we are back and everything is…" He allowed his words to trail into nothingness. "I have no expectations of you becoming…"

"Your mistress?" Adama's voice was quiet.

Involuntarily, Ikem felt heat rush up to his face, then was furious at himself for his own reaction. "I wanted to be clear about the fact that I don't. I wouldn't ever go as far as to say this never happened, but…you have nothing to fear from me. I will treat you with every professional courtesy going forward."

Adama actually laughed. "Professional courtesy?"

"Excuse me?"

"Ikem," she said. "Don't be a fool."

"Excuse me?" His blood ran hot again, but with anger this time.

"You saw me break down. We had sex," she said, emphasizing the word. "You've stripped me naked, explored every inch of my body. You've heard me plead with you."

Emotion pulsed in her voice, emotion that he'd not known she had the capability of showing until very recently.

"Adama—" he said, his own note of pleading entering his voice.

She shook her head. "I appreciate what you've said, but—" She pressed her lips together.

"What did you want me to say?" Ikem demanded. "I respect you too much to keep you as a mistress. You should be free from that kind of life, free to marry—" At the last word he choked a little. The sudden mental image of Adama, full breasts and slim waist and curved hips succumbing to the caresses of a man—*any* man—

"Kadir would be good for you," he found himself saying, and the look of absolute revulsion on her face made his heart constrict within his chest.

"Kadir?"

"Adama—"

"Perhaps you should have stopped talking when you assured me you wouldn't subject me to sexual harassment," Adama said coldly, "instead of trying to pimp me to your second-in-command!"

"I meant—not *him*, gods, he's like a father to both of us. I meant someone *like* him, Adama. Steady. Self-assured. Uncomplicated—"

Air hissed against her teeth, and she turned her head.

What was supposed to be a tender goodbye had quickly descended into something else entirely. He sighed, looked down at his feet, then back up.

"May I hold him?" he asked, reaching out for Adim. The baby strained toward him eagerly, and Adama handed him over, her lovely face neutral and cold as it was the first day he'd met her. Adim gurgled and squirmed, and Ikem sighed, then kissed him on the cheek. Adama's face softened—just a bit, but it was something.

"I'm sorry you can't come back with me," he told the baby, then chucked him under his chin and handed him back.

"What will you do with Adim after you return?" Adama said after a beat.

He lifted his shoulders. "I don't know. It depends on what happens to Felicité. I don't want him anywhere near that shoddy excuse for a mother. If Felicité chooses to stay, even if there was any involvement—I will pardon her."

Adama's brows lifted in surprise, and he shrugged again. "It would not behoove me to blame the mother for the sins of the daughter. And as Adim grows older, he's going to want to know things about his family that I can't provide answers for."

"He is very fortunate to have you, sir." She paused. "As was I, for a few days."

Ikem felt his throat constrict unexpectedly at her words, and he did not respond immediately; instead, he watched as she lifted her small chin.

"Kadir's waiting," she said.

"He is." Ikem hesitated for a fraction of a moment before bending to kiss her on both cheeks in the manner of court greetings, then on her mouth, a soft caress that lingered just enough for him to feel even when he'd pulled back again.

"Have you any advice for my rule?" he said, trying for a lightness he did not feel.

Adama bit her lip. "Do you mean it?"

"I wouldn't ask it if I didn't mean it."

She hesitated, then spoke, tucking a tendril of hair from her braid behind her ear. "You're a good man, Ikem. Trust your instincts. And remember that this is your throne, not your brother's. Take the time to listen to your own heart as well as that of the people you now rule. That will tell you what to do."

CHAPTER NINETEEN

IF THE SUN PALACE had been a gilded cage before, it was a citadel now, and one that Ikem couldn't even desire escaping. He simply didn't have the time.

Every morning, Ikem woke to the meticulous rituals of kingship, the smells of polishing wax and lavender water and starch and expensive teas. The murmured pronouncements of his advisers, deferential and cool, filled his ears both day and night. And he'd never felt so alone. Even Adim was gone now, living quietly and comfortably with his grandmother, watched carefully in a house at the edge of the capital. The old woman had been cleared of all conspiracy, and she'd humbly asked to stay.

"There's nothing for me back in my country, except a useless daughter," she'd said, and her lined face had been flushed with shame.

He'd granted her request. How could he not? And frankly, in the innermost parts of him, he wanted Adim close. His feelings for the little boy had not abated at all, though the familial ties had been dissolved.

He was king. He had the throne. And now he wasn't even sure where the throne ended and the man began.

Should he rule as Adim the Second had? To maintain the "wall of alliances," to keep the dissent at bay with carefully worded pronouncements? The thought made his stomach tighten; that hadn't worked out too well the first time, had it? With the border refugee disaster.

The reports from the border, no longer filtered by palace intermediaries, landed on his desk every morning even before his breakfast coffee. They were stark and damning.

He saw the suffering, the systematic cruelty of the Mwenye Mlimani's so-called food security reforms. He sat with a highlighter and notebook, grimly reading every word, taking note of every incident. And as he did it was as if Adama's quiet, firm voice was over his shoulder, detailing the routes, the villages, the human cost. He remembered the feeling of her hand in his, as they pored over intelligence reports together.

Together. It was odd, wasn't it? Missing someone you'd spent so little time with. But—they'd fit, as easily as if they were breathing from the same set of lungs, walking on the same set of legs. Sometimes that day it felt as if they'd shared a brain. And then, at night—

When those thoughts came he sometimes had to close his notebook, lock his computer and go for a walk. Not a run this time; his thoughts no longer skewed agitated after becoming king. He was slower, more deliberate in everything.

He often saw Adama, a flash of her uniform in the palace corridors, a glimpse of her stern, beautiful face. Her induction into the King's Guard was planned for the next couple of weeks; Kadir was putting her through the paces, and Ikem watched as much as he could without letting her know he was. She passed the requisite exams easily; she excelled in tests of hand-to-hand combat; she was as competent as ever, as fiercely disciplined. Ikem was so proud his heart nearly burst.

And he missed her. Gods, how he missed her. The sharp mind, the honesty, the contrast between a soldier's stoicism and a face that could be as open and as readable as a child's.

He thought of her as he spent hours poring over new data on Kijamii, consulting obscure texts on governance, speaking to the same old scholars he'd previously dismissed as *dull*. He was trying to find his own way, a third path between his brother's rigid traditions and that hellcat Catherine Elimu's sometimes radical demands.

It was a solitary journey, and the weight of it threatened to consume him.

He missed her very much. But time would ease it, he told himself. It was the only thing he could do.

"Your duty is to yourself, Your Majesty," Kadir told him one day during a quiet audience. "To the man you truly are. Not the man your brother was. Not the man you believe you must become." He paused. "She saw it, you know."

Ikem finally turned, his gaze sharp. "She?"

Kadir just looked at him, his dark eyes knowing. "She sees the king you were always meant to be. The one who cares for the people, not just the alliances. And I have full confidence in you, sir."

Ikem had almost disgraced himself by welling up that day.

He thought of Adama, of her mother's courage, of the unnamed faces at the border. He thought of his father's pride and its crushing effect on his brother. He thought of the mistakes that had been made.

He would not rule from a place of fear or a dead man's shadow any longer. He would rule from the heart he had almost forgotten he possessed.

* * *

The Sun Palace fairly reflected nervous, anxious energy these days, and Ikem found the early days of his kingship busier than he ever could have imagined.

The news from the Kijamii border was no longer just rumor. In response to the sanctions the Mwenye Mlimani's brutal reforms had escalated, driving a new, desperate wave of refugees across the mountains, overwhelming the border villages, including those Adama's mother protected. Calls for intervention, for more sanctions, now echoed not just from Catherine, but from the streets of Anwu's capital.

The entire country spoke of nothing else, and the very air they breathed was thick with tension. Would there be war? Would there be conflict?

Adama witnessed it all from her new position in the Royal Guard's strategic command; as part of her training for induction into the King's Guard, she'd been assigned to reviewing new security protocols for the aid convoys, overseeing intelligence on the Kijamii internal situation. She was wary of the position at first, but Ikem seemed determined to keep her at ease. She never saw him without a group of the other soldiers on her team, and when she did he was as cool and remote as the Anwuan moon, and—at least, to her—glowed just as brightly.

A fierce pride, raw and unfamiliar but not unwelcome, swelled within her with every encounter. Ikem's handsome face was still taut and lined with the burdens of leadership, but there was new light behind his eyes, a quiet strength that had quite transformed him. She remembered those early days, the defensive, agitated stance barely covered under the mantle of a regency that was as unwanted as it was ill fitting. Now he wore the weight of kingship as a rightful owner, not an interloper.

He'd shed the weight of Adim the Second's misery, and he was better for it.

Ikem did look at her sometimes. It was a gaze that lingered, deep and knowing, but he never approached. Not once since that painful, final conversation they'd had. And that chasm between them had become an ache with sharpness that would dull one day.

Hopefully, one day soon.

She hugged the ache at night in the barracks when she was alone, when the lights were off and she could admit to herself what she couldn't in the light of day. Sometimes she thought of him as she trailed between her thighs with cool fingers and in the gasping, damp aftermath she felt so completely bereft.

She'd pushed him away to avoid the hurt that came with closeness—but—wasn't this worse in a way? This longing, this all-consuming wonder about what might have been? She'd come into Ikem's household with the goal of getting what she wanted and leaving. Now a few weeks with him had shown her that perhaps she didn't know what she wanted that well, after all.

Perhaps she wanted to heal. But she had no idea how to go about that. And her induction into the Guard was upcoming, with a meeting alone with the king, as tradition demanded.

Alone with Ikem, whom she hadn't spoken to alone even once since they'd been back. Ikem, who consumed her thoughts during the day and her dreams in her bed at night. She no longer dreamt of her brother, but instead woke with aching breasts and wet thighs and she swore she could feel traces of the roughness of his hands on her skin.

She was going crazy.

The week before her induction, the king called a meeting with his advisers and the King's Guard. Kadir sent her a message requesting her presence.

"I'm not inducted yet, though," she protested.

"It's at the king's request," Kadir said, then looked at her in that odd penetrating way he'd adopted in recent days, since they'd come back from her mother's home. She did not question either the request or the look; she had a strong feeling it would take her down roads she had no desire to travel. Instead, she bowed her head in assent, and on the day of the meeting, donned her uniform, pinned her hair at the base of her neck severely and set off, commanding herself to be a bit less of a fool, just for this morning.

The meeting was not in the intimidating formal council room where Adim the Second had usually presided.

Ikem had gathered them in the King's Terrace, that venue for their long-ago breakfast. He'd made it over into a smaller, more intimate strategy chamber, and the soldiers, flanking Ikem's ever-present team of advisers, walked in to find strong coffee rather than the increasingly hard to get tea, freshly baked bread, grilled white cheese, grilled vegetables and lamb. Soldier's rations, but served in the most elegant way imaginable.

Ikem sat at the head of the table, talking quietly to Catherine Elimu. The older woman looked deferential, but wary. She'd quieted in recent weeks; the initial sanctions had mollified her.

Adama, unable to eat anything, looked at Ikem, at the calm on his face. Would he retreat, as he once had, to maintain the *stability* his brother had so painstakingly built? Would he try to appease, to deflect? Or—

Adama jerked to attention as Ikem brushed crumbs off his hands and stood. It took a few minutes for the voices to stop, for every piece of clattering silverware to be laid on the plates. But it did, and when it was quiet Ikem spoke—simply, clearly, without ceremony.

"The time for vague condemnations is over," he announced, his voice firm. There was a new authority there, not born out of arrogance, but out of a cool assurance that comes from knowledge, from time. "We'll send direct humanitarian aid immediately, overland, through the mountain passes."

Every eye in the room was fixed on Ikem; it was as if he had paused them with a remote control. He kept going.

"Our own military assets will secure the routes. Furthermore, Parliament will draft legislation for targeted economic sanctions, as well as military warning, effective immediately, until the Mwenye Mlimani ceases his atrocities against his own people and allows international observers."

A stunned silence. Then, Catherine's eyes, narrowed and sharp, met his. There was no triumph there, only a dawning respect. "Your Majesty…"

"This is not a political maneuver, Prime Minister," Ikem stated, his gaze sweeping the room, meeting every eye. "This is the only course for a nation that values its people and its soul." He cleared his throat. "I can't promise that this won't lead to conflict. But it is what we have to do."

It was still quiet, so quiet that Adama was sure her thudding heartbeat could be heard by all present. Ikem's face was unreadable—that is, until she stood to her feet, met his eyes and lowered her head into a bow.

He looked at her then, and it was as if her whole body was bathed in liquid flame.

As if choreographed, everyone else followed, and the first to do so was Catherine Elimu.

And later, after glasses were risen, Ikem left the King's Terrace to head back to his rooms.

Ikem could not remember the last time he felt so weary, so drained. The sleepless nights were beginning to catch up to him, and the adrenaline that had propelled him through his speech and this entire meeting had left with the swiftness with which it came, leaving him vaguely nauseated. The greasy spread left behind was wholly unappetizing; all he wanted was the largest jug of ice water the kitchen could procure, some ibuprofen and a quiet, dark room. He flexed his hand gingerly; it felt bruised from the endless pumps of well-wishers, sycophants, critics, allies.

He could not be tired, not now. He'd proven he was his own king. He'd made a start, maybe. He felt good about his decisions.

But now he was alone.

Ikem eased out of the doorway, practically ripping the diadem from his head; the chamber was pleasantly cool, with fresh air rushing down from the latticed windows close to the ceiling. His chambers would be even cooler. Ikem's fingers went to his collar, unbuttoning, loosening, tugging—

And then he stopped, for Adama stood there in the corridor, her hands tucked behind her—and—she looked—

Adama.

Who the hell was he kidding? She looked wonderful; he drank her in as if she were the water his parched throat wanted. And in that moment, his heart tightened within his chest, and he knew. He saw the depth of his feelings for her as if they'd been written in capital letters and placed on a signboard.

Adama stood sentinel-straight, silhouetted against the

faint light spilling from a distant sconce. The shadows clung to her, but her face was clear. Soft. Open in a way he'd never seen before. And unbelievably, she began to twist her hands together.

"Your Majesty," she began, then faltered.

She'd been waiting for him. And Ikem's composure, honed over weeks of isolation and rigid self-discipline, was already threatening to splinter. What she'd said—

Ikem, I don't have anything to give you. I wish I did, but I don't.

You... You'd demand everything. You wouldn't mean to, but you would.

And this—this was what terrified Ikem the most, because he knew precisely what that looked like, and he never wanted to put a woman he loved in that position.

He'd seen what it had done to him, after all.

That realization clashed with other memories, though. There was the sound of her laughter, her pain, the raw, aching slide of her body against his. The vulnerability. The desire. He remembered the clarity she brought to his muddled thoughts, the tenderness that flooded him when she was close.

His feelings about her were the first act of honesty he'd allowed himself in so long. And now there was something mirrored in those liquid eyes that made him swallow.

"Adama?"

She gestured, almost helplessly. "I—I'm not sure why I'm here, to be honest. I just—"

He took a step forward, then another. The sound of his dress boots on the polished floor echoed in the quiet corridor. When he stopped they were so close she had to tilt her head upward to look at him.

"I don't know why I'm here," she whispered.

He'd never wanted to touch her more, to span her small, muscled waist with his hands, to pull her flush against his body. From the look on her face he was fairly sure he wouldn't be rejected, either. He tilted his head down; his eyes flickered over the lush fullness of her mouth.

"You have a private audience with me soon, do you not?"

There was a cloudiness in her eyes that cleared a little. "I—"

"For your induction. Into the King's Guard." He did drop a hand to her hip then—he could not resist any more than he could keep from breathing. It brought to mind another night, not so long ago, although it seemed like another lifetime. Them, alone, in a corridor much like this one. Her soft, naked skin. Slow, hot kisses. Wet, dark nipples hardening against his mouth. And the start of an intimacy that felt realer than anything he'd experienced this year.

"Ikem," she said, and her voice was low and trembling. He did brush his lips with hers then, but it was barely a touch; he forced himself to draw back.

"Your induction," he said, and his voice was crisp, though thickened with desire so he could barely recognize himself. "We will talk there."

He turned and left her, his heart throbbing low in his chest.

Adama dressed for her official audience with Ikem with hands that trembled, in the military robing room of a palace that buzzed with new energy.

So much had happened in the past day and a half. News of King Ikem's decisive actions at the border had swept through Anwu like a cleansing fire. He had listened to the people, not just the old guard. He had become his own king. A fierce pride, both raw and unfamiliar, swelled within her.

He was their king. And she wanted him. She didn't know how it would look, or what it would come to, but she knew that if—that if he asked—

She would say yes. She'd give in without hesitation. And now she was in the barracks, cleansing herself slowly, methodically. Removing the hair from her body. Anointing herself with perfumed oils. Covering that scented softness with her new uniform, starched and tailored to perfection.

She could be both, she thought. Both soldier and lover. Ikem had given her that possibility, and finally, she was allowing herself to explore it.

Uzo arrived with her summons right on time, as the sun began dipping behind the trees, singing into the Ceres Mountains in the distance. Adama smiled to see him, remembering her first day waiting in the Obelisk Gardens and what it had led to. He made her a formal bow.

"Congratulations, ma'am."

He handed her the ceremonial torch, sputtering in the darkness, and she began to make the traditional walk alone. Her boots echoed down the long, lapis-tiled hallway; the lights were low in the palace this evening, for the induction. No one stood in the hallway; they were all hidden from sight. The King's Guard had to make this journey alone.

And then—she was at Ikem's wing of the palace, and at his door. He must have been anticipating her arrival, because the door creaked open, and he took the torch from her.

"Lieutenant Ohi."

She was so distraught she could barely answer. "Your Majesty."

"Are you willing to serve the Crown as one of the King's Guard?" It was a simple question, one intended to preface a meal with the king and finally, the ring of the King's Guard, fashioned from a lump of gold that had been in the Anwu treasury for generations. But there was so much more behind his question; she could read it in his eyes.

"I am," she whispered. "But what would it mean for me?"

Ikem's face grew troubled and thoughtful; then he leaned in and kissed her.

The kiss was slow and sweet; it was passionate without being angry, heated without being accusatory. It was the kiss of a man who trusted her; a lover's kiss. When he pulled back he caressed her face for a fraction of a moment; then he turned and began to walk.

"Come," he said over his shoulder.

As if drawn by some magnetic force, Adama walked after him. She had to hurry to match his long strides; it was her first time in his private apartments and he passed a banquet room, a receiving room, a small library, a gym. When he reached the final door he stopped, then pulled his tunic over his head in one smooth motion.

Adama's heart leaped into her throat, and she took a full step back. "Ikem—"

He turned his back to her.

His inner shirt was next, then his trousers. Adama felt her mouth go dry as he shed each layer, revealing gleaming skin and taut muscle. By the time he straightened, he was completely naked save for white linen shorts that hung low on his hips; when he turned she swallowed hard. The fabric did nothing to hide him, or the way he strained for her.

"You are beautiful, Your Majesty." And there it was, that choking sensation in her throat again. She blinked.

"So are you. Beautiful and bold and far too over-dressed," he said, then reached for her hand, tugged it to brace against his chest, right where his heart was beating. It was a strong, steady thrum, pulsing beneath smooth, warm skin. "Can you feel my heart racing, Adama? You do this to me."

"Ikem," she began, and to her horror her voice did crack then. There was a suspicious wetness beginning at the corners of her eyes; Ikem saw it and his face softened.

"If my words will not persuade you, then…" He lifted his shoulders. "I am naked before you, Adama. I am at your mercy."

"You cannot give me that kind of responsibility."

He smiled, a small smile that barely lifted the corners of his mouth; then he leaned forward, claimed her trembling lips with so much tenderness that she thought, in one wild moment, she might die from the longing that cramped her body.

Ikem took his time with the kisses; they were so gentle, so slow, that Adama thought she might go quite mad. He'd mocked her, angered her and teased her in moments like this, but never had he utilized this kind of deliberate gentleness, not to this degree. Between her legs, she tightened around the emptiness that was there; she wanted him, and she wanted him now.

"Ikem, please," she whispered. She barely felt it when his hands went to her waist, but she was aware when they slid beneath her clothing and touched her skin; each finger left a warm impression, a tingle of heat.

"Marry me," he commanded, and she felt her knees grow weak. His lips descended to her neck, her shoulder;

he whispered the words, branding them on her skin. His hands went behind her, found the fastenings; there was a tug and a jerk, and she was stepping out of the pool of heavy fabric, feeling as if ten pounds had been lifted from her shoulders.

"I can't," she moaned, but he was fumbling at the door of his bedroom, that iron control virtually gone. He swore under his breath, then managed to kick the door open.

"I'm completely helpless around you," he muttered, and then Adama was on her back, uniform shirt tugged over her head, naked skin sliding against silk and velvet, with the heat of his body pressing her down, a welcome pressure that would build, hard and fast and certain, to the pleasure they both were chasing.

Ikem did not concentrate on her body alone this time; he whispered words. Promises. Declarations that made her skin hot, made her cheeks burn. And finally, when she said those words back, small and broken, clinging to his neck as if he were a lifeline, he cried out in mingled pleasure and triumph.

Later, the two sat up to their necks in water so hot steam filled the air. The baths were Ikem's favorite part of his chambers; they featured a fountain of warm water poured on hot rocks, then flowing, steaming and hissing, into a pool. There was a second pool of lukewarm water, then a third of cold. Now sated, he could enjoy the sight of Adama's gleaming skin and full breasts, only partially obscured by the bath. She was still breathing a little unsteadily after their hurried, passionate coupling; her face looked troubled. She always looked troubled whenever she should relax, he thought wryly. He felt curiously weightless. He relaxed his body completely, floating to the top of the water.

"Were I not the king," he said, "would you marry me?"

Adama moved uncomfortably; ripples broke the surface of the water. "I don't want to marry anyone, Ikem."

"Why not? You might enjoy it."

"Because a relationship with you means I lose my freedom," she said after a moment. "I'm not afraid of having children anymore. Adim showed me that. But any children we might have…" Her voice trailed off.

Ikem's body went hot at the thought of Adama's supple body, swollen with his child. "Are you—"

"No." Her voice was calm. "But we must be practical, Ikem. I—I watched my brother die. I heard his screams grow fainter and fainter until he was gone. I ruined their lives, my parents' marriage—"

"Adama," he murmured.

"How could I be a good partner, or a good mother, with that hanging over my head?" she whispered. "It hurts like *hell*, Ikem."

He was silent for a long moment; then he drew her wet, naked body close and tight, ripples breaking the fragrant water. "I'm not better off, Adama. I watched my brother suffer in a marriage dictated by political strategy. I've been tied by duty, and you by guilt." He pressed a gentle kiss to her hair. "We chose solitude, didn't we? But we were wrong."

Her eyes filled, and he kissed her again.

"I love you," she whispered, and her heart was on her lips.

"And I, you."

Later, they lay tangled in the silk and velvet sheets of Ikem's bed, the last vestiges of desire still shimmering, fading into the deep, contented hum of sated bodies, weakened by lovemaking. Adama felt the steady thrum of Ikem's heart beneath her ear, the warmth of his hand stroking her back, tracing patterns along her spine.

So much had happened—so much. And for the first time in all her years of wandering she was content to be still.

"Ikem?"

"Hmm?" He was almost asleep.

"Are you serious?" she whispered, her voice rough, barely trusting the question. "About…marrying me?"

He was instantly awake and raised himself slightly. His dark eyes, heavy-lidded with passion, finding hers. "Yes, every word." His thumb stroked her cheekbone. "But—Adama—it's not a prerequisite. I'll take you any way you'd like. We're meant—to be partners, my love."

"Ikem—"

"Think about it." His voice was a low rumble in his chest. "We could— By the gods, Adama, we could do so much together."

She inhaled a little, tilting up her head to look into his face.

"My brother's mistake was sacrificing his true self," he finished simply. "Mine…would be to deny mine, and deny us. And I want to build this new…thing on truth, not old ways of doing things. Anwu needs an heir, yes, but it needs us more. And I believe, Adama, that our future together will be far greater than any my brother or my father could have imagined."

There was such conviction in his voice that her eyes filled, and he kissed her again.

"I love you," she whispered against his mouth, before the resilience she'd built up over the years could choke them back. It was almost laughable; terrifying, liberating and laughable, and what else could she possibly say in that moment? It was written all over her.

"And I, you." He pulled back slightly, his gaze serious. "Don't you see, Adama? I don't need a consort. I need a partner."

"Ikem—"

"Your strength, your insight… Anwu needs it. I need it. This isn't about sacrificing your freedom. It's about using it, with me, to build something better."

"I know this. But—" Her voice faltered, and she closed her eyes to keep her composure. What he was offering was as warm and as good to her as a fire is on a winter day, so bright and hard to look at, and it made the shadows of her past seem even darker.

Possibility. *Hope.* A different future, and one where she wasn't alone.

"Adama?" Ikem's voice nudged at the edges of her consciousness. "Tell me."

Adama inhaled; the taste of old grief was sharp and metallic on the back of her tongue, threatening to crowd her words out, but she swallowed it down. What if she failed him? Not in statecraft—that she could do in her sleep—but in loving him. What if the girl who stood by and watched her brother die…who couldn't even run for help…

What if she sabotaged this? What if she was broken beyond repair?

"You'll become frustrated with me," she gritted. "Because I'm frustrated with myself. Every single day. You can't have that kind of emotional liability, Ikem."

And I'm terrified. Adama had fought and trained on every terrain imaginable, but this was new ground.

Ikem's face grew hard, immovable. "Then we fail together," he said, his voice low and steady. "The king who ruled as a ghost and the soldier who was afraid to speak," he added, his mouth twitching a little. "We'll be a—" he struggled to find the words "—a beautiful disaster, Adama. And we will figure it out. Together." He leaned in, his forehead resting against hers, and his mouth tilted up a little. "My love…"

Her traitorous heart jumped more than a little at the endearment—it just sounded so right. "Yes?"

"Just think about it. Who could be better to protect a kingdom than someone who knows what it's like to lose everything?"

And it all came to Adama then, in bits and pieces, with all the warm, gentle softness of Anwu's spring breezes.

Your greatest shame can become your greatest strength.

Shared purpose. Shared partnership.

No longer a need to wander; finally being found.

A queen.

The last two words made her shiver a little; not from fear or disgust, but awe. Curiosity. And when Ikem drew her close she wrapped her own arms round him, tucking her head into the curve between his shoulder and his neck.

A warrior, a woman, a queen. Maybe a mother one day.

She wasn't losing herself; she was finally being found.

"Adama?" Ikem's voice rumbled low.

"Two conditions," she said, swallowing past her thudding heartbeat.

"Go on." There was apprehension mingled with the touch of amusement that always seemed to be there with her.

"I know we have to have a state wedding. Tradition—"

"Hang tradition," Ikem said fiercely. "I'm king. We can do what we want—"

"Let me finish." She placed gentle fingers on his lips. "It has to happen. We both know this. But—grant me a year. I'll marry you now, but grant me a year before a public celebration. And another before you crown me."

"Adama—"

"I need time, Ikem." She swallowed. "There's much that's still broken. It will be mended, I promise—especially with you to support me. But I need time."

Ikem shifted her to the cradle of his thighs; he wasn't aroused now; he was warm, comfortable, a support for her weary back. He began toying with the fluffy ends of her braids, his breath warm and sweet on her ear. "A year," he said, his voice thick. "Or two. Or ten. Or a lifetime. Whatever you need, Adama. I'm not going anywhere."

"Thank you," she whispered and relaxed fully on him. "Then—it's a yes."

"I have a condition, too."

She half turned around; he was smiling wryly. "What is it?"

"Kiss me first," he said.

She did, slanting her mouth against his with no hesitation whatsoever, the now-familiar stirrings of affection warming her skin. The kiss was a tender one, a loving one; one that held all the promises of the future.

"My condition," he murmured against her lips, "is that you never call yourself broken again. A partnership needs two whole people, Adama. And you were never anything less. You're the strongest person I have ever known."

For once, Ikem spoke words like that, and Adama took them as a prophecy. She didn't refute him in any way; instead, she brought his hands to the softness of her breasts,

And in that moment—in that intimate, scented, heated moment—the soldier who had wandered the world looking for a war to win finally laid down the last of the weapons in her arsenal.

She was home.

* * * * *

Were you blown away by Her Forbidden Royal Boss? *Then why not explore these other sizzling stories by Jadesola James!*

Redeemed by His New York Cinderella
The Royal Baby He Must Claim
The Princess He Must Marry
Billion-Dollar Ring Ruse

Available now!

Get up to 4 Free Books!

We'll send you 2 free books from each series you try
PLUS a free Mystery Gift.

Both the **Harlequin Presents** and **Harlequin Medical Romance** series feature exciting stories of passion and drama.

YES! Please send me 2 FREE novels from Harlequin Presents or Harlequin Medical Romance and my FREE gift (gift is worth about $10 retail). I may cancel anytime by emailing ReaderServiceInfo@Harlequin.com or by calling 1-800-873-8635. If I don't cancel, I will receive 6 brand-new larger-print novels every month and be billed just $7.19 each in the U.S., or $7.99 each in Canada, or 4 brand-new Harlequin Medical Romance Larger-Print books every month and be billed just $7.19 each in the U.S. or $7.99 each in Canada. That's a savings of 20% off the cover price! It's quite a bargain! Shipping and handling is just 75¢ per book in the U.S. and $1.75 per book in Canada.* I understand that accepting the free books and gift places me under no obligation to buy anything—they are mine to keep for free no matter what I decide.

Choose one:
- ☐ **Harlequin Presents Larger-Print** (176/376 BPA G3CD)
- ☐ **Harlequin Medical Romance** (171/371 BPA G3CD)
- ☐ **Or Try Both!** (176/376 & 171/371 BPA G3CE)

Name (please print)

Address   Apt. #

City   State/Province   Zip/Postal Code

Email: Please check this box ☐ if you would like to receive newsletters and promotional emails from Harlequin Enterprises ULC and its affiliates. You can unsubscribe anytime.

> Mail to the **Harlequin Reader Service:**
> **IN U.S.A.:** P.O. Box 1341, Buffalo, NY 14240-8531
> **IN CANADA:** P.O. Box 603, Fort Erie, Ontario L2A 5X3

Want to explore our other series or interested in ebooks? Visit www.ReaderService.com or call 1-800-873-8635.